D0533675

This book is due for return on or before the last date shown
above: it may, subject to the book not being reserved by
another reader, be renewed by personal application, post, or
telephone, quoting this date and details of the book.

HAMPSHIRE COUNTY COUNCIL
County Library

100%
recycled paper

Books by the same author

The Burning Baby and Other Ghosts
Catch Your Death, and other stories
The Ghost on the Hill
The Grasshopper
The House on the Brink
Ordinary Seaman (autobiography)
The Spitfire Grave and other stories
The Waterfall Box

GILRAY'S GHOST

JOHN GORDON

WALKER BOOKS
AND SUBSIDIARIES
LONDON • BOSTON • SYDNEY

First published 1995 by Walker Books Ltd
87 Vauxhall Walk, London SE11 5HJ

This edition published 1996

2 4 6 8 10 9 7 5 3 1

Text © 1995 John Gordon
Cover illustration © 1995 Julek Huller

This book has been typeset in Sabon.

Printed in England

British Library Cataloguing in Publication Data
A catalogue record for this book is available
from the British Library.

ISBN 0-7445-4389-4

For Frank and Maggie

1

'Twas brillig, and the slithy toves
Did gyre and gimble in the wabe
— Lewis Carroll, "Jabberwocky"

Deep within the forest a light flickered briefly through the bushes and vanished. Gilray, who could fly when he put his mind to it, lifted himself to chair-height above-ground for a better vantage point. He had been closing on the uncertain light for some time and did not want to lose it, but now he saw only that the deep gloom ahead of him was intensified by the criss-crossing of black branches. All was still.

He grumbled as he held his position among the lower branches, lapsing into baby talk, mothering himself, for he was alone and afraid. "Did I hear voice of young girl? Was it girlie-wirlie I heard in deep, dark woods? No, I think not. This place too lurksome for young lady at night."

He sank to earth. It was a summer night but he

wore an overcoat, and the energy he had used in raising himself made him sweat. He tilted his hat to the back of his head so that he could wipe his brow, and he leant against the tree. Silence wound itself around him as if it would bind him to the trunk, and the longer he stood the more difficult it was to move.

The night had become so soundless that when the light showed itself again, far off, it was as sharp as a distant cry. Then it vanished, as if it had shown itself only to emphasize that now he was utterly alone and in the dark.

Gilray, moving as if the wrinkles in his clothing creaked like hinges, settled his hat more squarely on his head, the brim now cool on his brow, and drew a deep breath. He was listening so intently for the sounds of hidden watchers creeping towards him that panic began to eat at his will and he doubted his ability to float clear of the ground. With a great effort he closed his eyes and concentrated.

Panic came galloping in again, but as it did so the pressure on the soles of his feet lessened. Then a leaf scraped the brim of his hat and flicked by his face, and relief surged through him with such power that he rose too swiftly and the rush of his ascent made a roosting pheasant scream and batter its way through the treetops.

Gilray paused, hovering among the branches, listening until the pheasant settled and left the night to him. He began to swim through the trees.

The summer canopy made dim caverns through which he glided, silent for the most part and brushing the foliage so gently that any listener on the forest floor would have looked up only at the grunts he made as he hauled himself over a thick branch and kicked forward. But there was no one to see his bulky form drifting like a dark cloud, and no more birds cried out to mark his progress.

He knew the tomb existed, and where it was to be found in the heart of the forest, but he almost drifted by without seeing it. The flickering light, like a will-o'-the-wisp, had led him astray. He had been so certain that whoever carried the light had been heading for the tomb that he had been thrown off course when the night-walker struck away in another direction. And now, hardly knowing by what route he had got there, he had blundered into the clearing.

He sighed as he hung among the topmost branches, fingering the leaves to keep from rocking. "All is safe," he murmured. "No nasty work this night."

There was relief in his voice, but he was nevertheless cautious. He looked down. Only the top of the tomb showed, the tip of its pyramid, and even that was overshadowed by the trees which rose above it. Bushes obscured its base, and ivy shrouded its sloping sides.

He regarded it for a long time, sing-songing, "Silent for a century. A slow century gone by. Forgotten-otten-otten," until he sighed as if at last he had achieved something long wished for and said, "I am not too late."

He began to sink towards the ground, but never for a moment allowing his eyes to stray from the pyramid. As its peak rose above him, his breathing quickened and fear began to grip him once more.

"No. No. No," he chanted breathlessly, denying some thought that troubled him, and when his feet settled silently into a patch of long grass he found comfort from his gentle landing. "Softly, softly. Very comfy."

Once more he listened, but the only sound he could detect was the faint cry of the stars as they spun in the heavens, still busy with creation. Down here, the forest and the pyramid were silent. "Peace," he murmured. "All's peacefulness."

He went forward, retaining sufficient weight-lessness to barely disturb the grass with his footsteps, and began to circle the pyramid. It was no more than the height of a house but its leaf-covered bulk dominated the forest floor. There was a portal. He could see the wedge of an opening cut into one of the pyramid's sides and he moved towards it until, through a screen of ivy, he saw that its heavy iron door was still in place. He pushed at it, but it was shut fast. "Peace and niceness," he whispered. "All's well."

He stooped to examine the stone kerb below the door. "No sign of visitors this night. No torch-bearers came this way." He laughed softly and chided himself. "No need for alarm, stupid man."

Nevertheless he continued to circle the pyramid, examining the ground as if looking for a trail. There was none.

Bushes grew thick along the pyramid's foot and reached up almost to obscure the dark shadow of another opening in its side. At first sight this seemed to be another entrance but was, in fact, a window slot to shed light into the interior of the mausoleum. Its sill was at ground level and it was unglazed, but the opening was protected by a grille of iron bars.

Gilray pushed the branches of the crowding bushes aside and leant towards the opening. He bent down and let the fingers of one hand brush the sill, delicately stroking the tufted moss and the few dried leaves that lay there, but they had not been recently disturbed. "All still for ages and ages, amen," he whispered, expelling his breath until, with emptied lungs, he put his face into the shadow of the opening and breathed deeply.

What he detected made him moan and draw back, rocking to and fro, and chanting to himself.

"Ghostie, ghostie, little ghostie," he sang. "Unsweet scent of ghostie doth tarnish rock and rot grass." He crouched and sniffed the ground. "Is pure decompose of centuries. Is freshly laid just here!"

Alarm made him bend double, snuffling at the ground, and then, clumsy and urgent, he moved forward on his knuckles as he picked up the trail. "Is strong!" he wailed as he stood upright and plunged into the forest. "Is strong!"

He made no effort any longer to be quiet as he thrashed through the trees, but suddenly he stood still, swaying his head from side to side as he sniffed the air. "Is gone!" He sampled the forest air carefully. "Ghostie gone home." His alarm subsided. "Good night, foul beastie, good night."

His shoulders drooped wearily, but as he turned to trudge back towards the pyramid something still troubled him. "What brought you out tonight, old spook, you scavenge hound?" His voice was a murmur. "Not me. Too old, too tough for thee, my friend. Thou hast need of sweeter meat."

Once more he stopped short and looked down. He had cleared the overhang of the trees and was crossing an open patch. There was no path, but even in the dimness he was aware that here and there the long grass showed a line as if it had recently been parted.

"Human man hath here been walking! Recent, recent, recently gone by!" From stooping he jerked upright, sensing the air again, once more trembling. "And girl! Young girlie-wirlie. The perfume of her garment doth enrich the night." He loosened his tie and unfastened his collar. "Who she?" he said. "Who?"

The gleam of the torch-bearer had long since disappeared into the forest gloom but, moving faster now, Gilray went in pursuit, willing himself clear of the ground once more and crying "Who? Who? Who?" as he rose.

2

June, and many a scythe in sunshine flames
                    – Matthew Arnold, *The Scholar-Gipsy*

"I wasn't scared," said Linda Blake, "until the stupid torch gave out."

"I wouldn't have gone there in the first place." Her companion had a face which had never lost the smooth outline of a child's, and hair as tawny as a wheatfield bleached by the sun. "I am too much of a coward," she said.

"Gary was with me, don't forget," said Linda, and laughed in her throat. "Except that's a danger in itself. But honestly, Cassandra, if you'd heard that owl go who-hoo-hoo in that bloody old forest, you'd have been scared out of your pants – I was. Just about." She laughed again, and Cassandra Ashe blushed.

It was going to be a hot day. Already the air along the riverbank, where the two girls were walking to high school, was full of the drifting

13

motes of summer, falling petals wafting among drunken butterflies. A teacher, coming from behind, cycled past.

Cassandra said, "Good morning, Mr Wheatley."

Linda, calling after him, cried, "Hi, Bob!"

Freewheeling, he turned his head to look over his shoulder and banter with the two sixth formers. "See me after school, you two."

"OK, Bob," Linda called, "it'll be a pleasure."

He flapped his hand, having no answer for her familiarity, and cycled on.

"You embarrassed him," said Cassandra.

"He loves it," said Linda. "But don't they all? Especially him."

In the staffroom, Bob Wheatley lay back in his chair until he was practically horizontal. "My God," he said, and moaned softly. "They'll ruin me. They make me feel old – an aged, aged man."

"You look," said Jessica Gifford without raising her eyes from the stack of papers she had on her lap, "no worse than usual. Which is to say, disgusting."

"You know I am in love with you, Jessica."

She marked another paper and laid it aside, ignoring him.

"Why are you so dismissive?" he asked.

"Dismissive is good," she said. "I like dismissive. It's exactly how I feel about you. Dismissive. Thank you, Mr Wheatley, it's something to remember you by."

14

He reclined, hands linked on chest, tie loosened, and regarded her. She had a beautifully smooth face – smooth *and* beautiful, he thought, expanding, as he often did, the first words to come into his mind. And her black eyebrows arched with the same exquisite swell as her breasts. "That Linda Blake girl is going to get someone into trouble one day," he said.

"Probably you." She spoke without interest, and paused in her marking to take an apple from the briefcase on the floor beside her.

"You mistake my train of thought, Jessica. She gave me the come-on just now, but I thought only of you."

"I am not flattered."

"She is dark, like you, and I – I mean men, all of them – find her very attractive."

"And you think she doesn't know it? You're a pushover for anything in a skirt, Bob Wheatley. It's a joke." She bit into her apple. He noticed, and she noticed him noticing, that she had very even and remarkably white teeth. "And don't you dare say 'lucky apple' every time I bite."

"May I think it, Miss Gifford?"

"Be my guest." She bit again.

"If you keep on doing that, Miss Gifford, I shall have to leave the room."

Her eyes were dark and healthy, her forehead perfect, and her black hair was held back by what would have been a simple ribbon except that it also was exotically black. She was as smooth and shiny as a Russian doll. He wanted to call her Olga, so he did.

"Olga," he said, "did you know your nose wrinkles ever so slightly every time you bite?"

She gathered her papers together and, without bothering to look his way, stood up. "Funny little man," she said.

"If I didn't have Gary," said Linda Blake, "I'd quite fancy Bob Wheatley, except he's a bit old ... and he's a teacher, of course, as well as being a bit of a prat."

"How old is Gary?" Cassandra asked, and then saw Linda looking sideways at her, suspecting cattiness. Gary was some years older than Linda. "What I mean," Cassandra added, confused, "is that he can't be anywhere near as old as Mr Wheatley."

"Put it this way," said Linda. "Gary is old enough to fancy my mum, and I know she goes for him, the old bat. My dad hates him."

"Well, he would, wouldn't he?" Cassandra knew she was expected to agree but she had to struggle to keep up with Linda's disdain for parents.

"So," said Linda, and stuck two fingers into the air, "that to my wonderful mother. Especially tonight."

"What about tonight?"

"I'm not supposed to tell you," said Linda, "so I will."

The two girls had arrived in front of school. The building, standing back, had once been the home of a Victorian banker and it still raised a haughty frontage as if the riverbank was private property. They lingered by the ornamental gates that stood at the entrance to the driveway.

"Tonight," said Linda, "we are going to the same place as last night, and you'll never guess why. It's because Gary has this kink. You know he's got stacks of horror stories and sex stuff in his car... "

It was the first Cassandra had heard of this taste of his, but she had no trouble believing it. The smell of Gary's aftershave had already told her. She nodded.

"Well, he's got on to something really, really local and he's all excited about it. There was an old person who used to live somewhere around here years and years ago and they reckon he used to do funny things with kids." Linda laughed. "Girls mainly; especially girls. So, naturally, loverboy's been going into it and he thinks he's found out where the old pervert is buried so he wants to go and have a look. With me – naturally."

"Why you?"

"Wake up, Cassandra! Because I'm not a boy, that's why. I'm led to believe I'm a girl. Female. And Gary thinks the randy old sod would like that and come for me."

"That's awful!"

"Isn't it, though!" Linda was delighted. "He

wants to use me as ghost bait."

"And you don't mind?"

"I love it."

Cassandra looked across the river. A few cars, glittering like beads, followed the curve of its bank as it swept through the town. They were a gigantic necklace. "I see," she said.

Linda sighed. "Sometimes, Cassandra, I wonder about you."

"I don't know what you mean."

"Oh, yes you do."

The two girls gazed at each other until Cassandra's eyelids fell. The other girl studied the soft outline of her mouth and the droop of her eyelashes before she said, "They're after you all the time, aren't they?"

"Who?"

"Boys. I'm talking about boys, stupid. And don't frown as though you don't know. Someone who looks like you has just got to know what they think."

Cassandra, embarrassed, shook her tawny hair. "Well, you don't do badly, either."

"Not as bad as I want to."

They both laughed.

"But isn't Gary a bit scary?" said Cassandra. "All those books and things."

"That means you don't like him, right?"

"I didn't say that! I hardly know him, do I?"

"Don't worry about Gary. He may be a weirdo, but he's only a man and I can cope with that. He's certain we nearly found the tomb last night, and he's just like a kid about it so we're going to have another go tonight. He's sure if we ever get near it I'll stir something up." She began to laugh as she trailed her hand along the wrought iron of the gate. "If you see what I mean."

3

Far from the fiery noon, and eve's one star,
Sat gray-hair'd Saturn, quiet as a stone
                                        – John Keats, "Hyperion"

It was noon when Bob Wheatley decided to cut his classes and cycle into town. The sky had been fired by the heat of the sun into blue enamel, and the rooftops trembled beneath it. In the marketplace he allowed the glare of the parked cars to hurt his eyes. Why not? – Jessica Gifford had called him a little man, and little he was. Taller than you, Jessica, but little, little, little.

Market Street was narrow and the shade was almost cool, but beyond it the curve of the Crescent caught the glare of the sun like a gigantic reflector and focused it on him. She had told him to run along and impress his sixth form girls – "your teen hareem" – and he cycled into the quietness of Museum Square knowing he was a beetle scurrying for shelter. In truth he had not even had the nerve to cut his classes; all he had done was to quit school during a free period and decide to forget he was on dinner duty. Big, big deal.

He chained his machine to the railings of the museum and climbed the steps to the slightly lopsided front door. The building was gently tilting into the fenland soil, and he was in harmony with it.

There was no one in the foyer, but the pages of the ancient bound volume of *The Fen Messenger* in its glass case showed the correct week and month as if its pages had flipped over like the flaps of a digital timepiece, running one hundred years late. "I wonder he bothers," Wheatley murmured as he walked towards the door of the curator's office. There was never anyone looking at *The Messenger*.

Fred Wherry was his own age, but married. Wheatley opened the office door. "It's me," he said. "Just going to the library." There was no one there. Wherry often slipped out for an odd half-hour, maintaining that his wife in the flat upstairs was looking after the shop. Wheatley went to the foot of the stairs and listened. Silence.

He was tempted to go up. Peg Wherry could be there alone. Once, just once, her small plump body had moulded itself to his and they had fumbled together. But that had been at the end of a party, in a dim corridor, and today he was sober. Anyway she was probably with her husband, or they might have gone out together. Everyone was

21

playing truant today. "Don't worry, I won't tell the trustees," he mumbled and walked across the foyer through the echo of his footsteps.

The library was in a wing of its own and closed to casual visitors, but Wheatley, because he was friendly with the Wherrys, had privileges. The large door swung softly, pushing into air scented with book dust. It was a refuge, and he breathed it in.

He had taken several paces before he became aware that he was not alone. From the very first moment his eyes had been fixed on another occupant, but had not registered him as human. It was not that this individual was in any way furtive; far from it – he was very noticeable, but in so unexpected a position that Wheatley had mistaken him, of all things, for a flag. The library was tall and narrow, which was why the figure suspended above ground against the end wall, spreadeagled against the books, had struck him as no more remarkable than a banner in a church. It was some relic of a regiment that Wherry had hung there.

The way the figure moved added to the deception. It was swaying slightly, oscillating as if caught in a gentle breeze. But suddenly, sickeningly, Wheatley realized what it was that he was looking at. The draped banner was a hanged man, and the library ladder further along the wall showed where he had stepped off.

"Dear God!" Wheatley's first flash of thought was to cut him down – but how? He shrank from it. It was impossible. It couldn't be done. The dead man was too far from the ground, too heavy, too repellently draped in an overcoat. And once the body was down he would have to dig the rope from the groove in the fat neck, stoop close and touch the corpse with his lips to breathe life into it. No, not that. But do something, Wheatley. Move.

He ran forward, barging a library table, scattering documents, and he was still staggering when the figure, hideously, jerked an arm. Worse, it began to swing around. Or at least its head turned itself in an idle fashion towards him. A globe of a pale white face, eyes forced open by the squeeze of the knot, gazed blankly back along the empty library.

Wheatley tugged at the ladder, and discovered it would not be long enough to reach. He looked up. He searched to find out how the man could have stepped upwards, beyond the top rung, in order to put his head through a noose. It was impossible. But then the swaying feet brushed a shelf and the toe of one scrubbed and patchy suede shoe pushed aside a book.

"Ah, yes!" The foot had made him understand, and he congratulated himself in order to remain calm. The shelves themselves formed a ladder.

Another sigh, but this time not from his own lips, disturbed the silence of the library. It was expelled from the dead lungs above his head.

In order to prevent himself turning and running Wheatley clutched at the ladder, but then his heart lurched as a voice echoed in the empty spaces.

"Quick! Quick!" The words made Wheatley twist to look over his shoulder, alarmed but desperately relieved that someone else had entered. Nothing, however, stirred in the long room. He was still alone, and the only sound was the scuff of the dead man's feet brushing the books.

"So very glad of your help!" Now the voice bounced down from the ceiling, and Wheatley jerked his head back.

Both feet of the hanged man, by some fluke, were now touching the top rung of the ladder. And then, either because the hidden rope was stretching or the neck was being elongated by the weight of the body, one foot came down delicately to the rung below.

"No!" Wheatley thrust himself back, rejecting what he saw. "No!"

"Why deny?" The voice came from the books above. The hands had risen to clutch the shelves, and the feet were descending the ladder.

"Your help is greatly appreciated, kindly sir. I had ventured too far along this bookish cliff face and was in danger of headlong descent." The figure paused and gazed down. "Onto my bonce."

The stranger was bulky, and Wheatley drew back, wary of someone more powerful than himself. But then the man, breathing as heavily as if he was, in fact, recovering from strangulation, stepped to the floor and in doing so revealed he was much shorter than Wheatley. He had a white and pudgy face, with the bridgeless nose of a doll, and he smiled as he introduced himself.

"Mr Gilray," he said, putting out a hand. "But please, for friendliness, omit mister."

"If you like." Wheatley's mind was on other things. "Just now," he said, "when I came in I thought you were in mid-air. Hanging ... I mean, suspended somehow."

Gilray giggled and raised his arms to claw the air. "Was clinging on for dear life. By skin of teeth." His plump face had an unwashed, natural sheen, and his porkpie hat and overcoat had obviously overheated him for, as he shook Wheatley's hand, his clasp was greasy. "Thank you so much for your aptly timed appearance, Mr Wheatley ... unless," his grin widened to show a snaggle of teeth, "I may call you just Wheatley, Wheatley?"

"You know me?"

"No astonishment necessary, Wheatley. Your chum the curator told me that a gent with your monicker would be along in search of romance."

Suddenly Wheatley wanted to laugh, and had to frown to prevent it. It was hardly typical of Fred, but he might have allowed a stranger to use the library. The slang, however, was too dated to be a copy of anything Fred might have said. And what could he have meant by saying that Wheatley was in search of romance? Had Peg said something? Did her husband know something of that heated, intimate moment? A trickle of alarm teased Wheatley's backbone.

Gilray's eyes narrowed wickedly. "You paled

like naughty man at sound of romance, Wheatley."

"What do you mean by that?"

"It was jocularity, Wheatley old boy. To make you laugh by hinting at hidden sex life." He himself laughed.

Wheatley, watching him, was not surprised that Gilray's snub of a nose looked as if it had been broken. Then, suddenly, understanding dawned. "You are in error about romance, Mr Gilray. The only romance that attaches to me is that I came here to study a poet – a Romantic. This one." He lunged suddenly past Gilray and plucked a small volume from among the leather-bound spines. "Keats," he said. "John Keats."

"Nice." Gilray reached for the book but Wheatley kept it clear of him. It was a copy of the 1820 poems, a first edition that Keats himself could have handled, and nothing would make him place it in the grubby palm presented to him. Gilray was unperturbed. "Mr Keats was small sexpot, one understands."

"If you like." Wheatley was beginning to turn away, annoyed by the interloper in the library.

"Little Johnny K. is ideal for lover of young ladies, however. Honeypot words and excessive swoonsomeness."

"Not for me," Wheatley said stiffly, putting a barrier between himself and this oddity who was ruining the loneliness he had hoped to engineer for himself. "I am a teacher. I teach."

Gilray nodded roguishly. "You are a favourite

of young ladies, nevertheless."

"How can you say that?"

"Scent of girl comes with you."

4

Summer ends now; now, barbarous in beauty,
  the stooks arise
Around; up above, what wind-walks! what lovely
  behaviour
Of silk-sack clouds!
            – G. M. Hopkins, "Hurrahing in Harvest"

Guilt about his stolen lunch hour made Wheatley avoid the staffroom and head straight for his form room behind the main building. The school had settled snugly into the banker's riverside mansion but now, like a hermit crab, it was outgrowing its shell so that Wheatley had to head out across the lawns to where he taught.

Immovable mobile classrooms made a caravan park of the banker's trees – the Bingo Beach. The name was frowned on, but the head had not been able to stamp it out. Wheatley climbed into his room. It was hot inside and he took off his jacket and loosened his tie in defiance of the head's version of Victorian values. He closed his eyes. The odour of chalk dust never changed, yet he enjoyed it. It was a secret vice, like the pleasure of learning.

There was a drum of feet on the wooden stairs outside and he called, "Come!", but just a fraction too late. The door had banged open without his invitation and the Arts Sixth slouched in, dropping their bags and sacks beside their desks. They were not, he knew, unduly aggressive, but nevertheless a dumb antagonism came with them.

"Welcome to the caravanserai," he said.

"Wha'?" said Piggins. "Whassat?"

"A place where camels rest, Piggins."

"Uh?"

"Precisely." By God, the youth looked like one, thick bottom lip hanging open, grunting. It was time for a counter-attack. Wheatley raised his voice. "No more masticating in class!"

Giggles, guffaws and shifts. Girls eyed boys sideways, and Piggins ostentatiously looked into the palm of his hand.

"There's no hair growing there, Piggins. Even if you are the greatest masticator ever known."

"Tha's an insult, sir."

"Spit or swallow, Piggins. Nobody chews while I talk." Wheatley did the swift sideways jink around his own desk that meant, or was meant to mean, business. On their feet, there were one or two of the boys who could match him for height but, slumped in their chairs, the advantage was his.

"Gerard," he said slowly.

29

"Manley," he added.

"Hopkins," he concluded.

He paused, looked at the ten faces and knew he had the attention of nine of them. Piggins was the problem. He had lifted his top lip to show his teeth and was gazing around at the others as if he had no idea what was going on.

"Yes, Piggins? Haven't you heard of Gerard Manley Hopkins, poet, priest and..."

"I thought you were calling the register, sir."

Some loyal giggles, but not many. Nat Woodburn, cleverer and much more dangerous than Piggins, seemed to have something on his mind. Well, who wouldn't, sitting next to a girl like that? Good luck to you, son, but I shall claim pedagogue's privilege and disturb your love life.

"Cassandra," said Wheatley, and the vision sitting next to Nat Woodburn raised her eyes to his. "You know something about Hopkins, I believe."

"A little bit," she said. "I read that poem you told us about last week." And more, much more, but she didn't care to give so much away. "I liked it."

He saw her timidity and shielded it by refusing even to smile. But, to hell with it, a face like that deserved a celebration. "'Look at the stars!'" he said suddenly, "'look, look up at the skies! O look at all the fire-folk sitting in the air! The bright boroughs, the circle-citadels there!'" He broke off, as startled with himself as the rest of them. "And that's a Victorian speaking," he said. "Hopkins."

30

"He doesn't sound old-fashioned," said Cassandra Ashe. "Not when you hear him, I mean. I think he's modern."

Lovely girl. Model pupil. She was dangerously beautiful, but now he dared risk a smile in her direction. "Dylan Thomas liked him."

"That is," Nat Woodburn broke in, "if you call Dylan Thomas modern." He had, as always, read beyond what was required of him.

"No need to sneer, Woodburn." Wheatley defended the girl, who was blushing. "If it's good, it's modern. Never mind all that crap about Victorian values you get pushed at you..." He had the class with him now. They grinned, recognizing his knock at the head's annual and notorious Founders' Day grovel in front of parents. "Hopkins was Victorian, but is it *Victorian* to write about 'brute beauty and valour and act'?... or of something being 'barbarous in beauty'..." He did not look at the girl.

Now that Mr Wheatley had begun to talk, carried away by words, saying far too much for his own good, Cassandra was able to look at him. With his tight curly hair and his lovely clean little ears, he was as golden brown as a bun, a Sunblest wholemeal loaf, Mr Kipling's exceedingly fine cakes, luscious and longlife, with just a wrinkle at the corner of his cornflower eyes to show his age, and a small golden corn stubble of a moustache to make him a... There was a word, but it had gone. A word he'd told her.

31

Wheatley glimpsed the tiny frown that tried, but failed, to cast a shadow in her startling eyes, and he said harshly, too harshly, "Yes, Cassandra?"

"It doesn't matter, sir. I was just thinking."

"A sixth former who thinks? *Mirabile dictu.*" There was a groan, and he turned away, apologizing. "Latin. I pray forgiveness for stretching your brains to such a radically painful extent. It's this man Hopkins, he's the miraculous speaker – he reaches beyond what is sayable, and says it. Cassandra, I think, knows that." He was not being fair to her; he was making her the victim of a schoolmaster's ploy to get someone on his side in order that the rest would follow. And then she moved. She wore a white blouse and, without meaning to, he said what was suddenly on his mind: "And is it *Victorian* to say of a woman's breasts 'what lovely behaviour of silk-sack clouds!'"

"Chroist!" said Piggins.

Hopkins, as far as anyone knew, had not had breasts in mind when he'd written those words, but Piggins would never know that. Wheatley turned to where the main threat lay. "Modern enough for you, Woodburn?"

And then Cassandra remembered the word. Mr Wheatley's tie was ever so slightly loosened, the top button of his shirt undone, and how tight the material of his shirt was over the muscles of his arm. He was bursting out; overflowing ... like a *cornucopia*!

He saw her shift her buttocks on her chair, and a redness gleamed suddenly in his already ruddy complexion. Sixteen … dear God, preserve me. He gritted his teeth and thought of Hopkins, a sufferer, ensnared by his religion and homosexuality.

5

From boy's pierced throat and girl's pierced bosom
Drips, reddening round the rose-red blossom,
  The slow delicious bright soft blood,
Bathing the spices and the pyre,
Bathing the flowers and fallen fire,
  Bathing the blossom by the bud.
                        – Algernon Charles Swinburne, *Ilicet*

Wheatley said it again. "He was climbing up the shelves without a ladder. I can swear to it."

Peg Wherry was laughing at him. "Poor Bob, it's the strain of teaching. It's making you hallucinate."

They were in the flat over the museum. Fred Wherry reached across the table and poured more wine into Wheatley's glass. "There isn't the slightest sign of damage – not a book out of place, not a footprint. But drink up and we'll go down and have another look."

"Don't bother. I'm used to people paying no attention to what I say – I teach, don't forget. But you ought to be careful who you let into this place. Whom." He groaned at having corrected himself, and Peg laughed again.

"Well, if we let the likes of you in here, Bob Wheatley," she said, "who can we keep out? Whom?"

They leant across the table until their foreheads almost touched and gargoyled at each other. "And where were you this morning," he said, "when I needed you?"

"Fred was out. I was up here alone."

"I called."

"Not loud enough," she said, and a sudden seriousness in her voice made them both realize she would have welcomed him.

If Fred Wherry noticed their sudden silence he did not show it. He was as self-contained as an android, chockfull of intellectual links, and his long, smooth face had few emotional synapses. They twitched now, however, into a smug smile. It meant he was about to be jocular, and Wheatley prepared himself.

"Won't you two rubes ever grow up?" Old movie-speak was a Wherry speciality. "That guy in the library was no knuckle-head; not one of your dime a dozen goofballs."

"Gee," said Wheatley. "Wowie." A sharp glance from Peg silenced him.

"OK, you kids, I'll be serious."

"We hang upon your every word." Wheatley did not glance at Peg.

"I expect you know," said Wherry, "that many ancient beliefs – of a magical nature, often enough – still reverberate in contemporary cultures."

Wheatley's attention strayed to the window. Across Museum Square, where the church tower was warming its stones in the setting sun, he could see the broken slats of the louvres through which pigeons fluttered into the gloom of the bell chamber. An easy life, a pigeon's. Coo-coo-ruckety-coo. Anyone with Fred's pomposity deserved to have his wife made love to by someone who spoke English. And then Fred's voice brought him back from pigeons.

"Were you aware," he said, "that no more than a spit from where we sit there's a mausoleum in pyramidal form where an ancient shaman, a magus, is interred, and where magical rites are said to presently take place?"

Wheatley winced at "presently", and said, "It's news to me, Fred."

"Your allegedly mad friend informed me."

"And you believed him?"

"I have had several conversations with Mr Gilray. I am quite satisfied he is a genuine student of such arcane matters."

"He's bonkers."

Wherry shrugged, and became more condescending. "Think about it," he said, and again his lips turned up to make a small, smug chevron on his long face.

Peg suddenly got up from the table and pulled

Wheatley to his feet. "And you," she said to her husband, "can come and show us what the madman found."

"Or didn't find." Wherry sat where he was. "His search was unsuccessful. His opinions were the only matter of interest."

"Sometimes, Fred," she said, "you are insufferable." She turned to Wheatley. "If he's not going to show you what they've been looking at, then I shall." At the door she gave her husband a last chance. "Are you coming?"

He waved a hand, dismissing them. "It's all old stuff, of no serious interest in itself. Help yourselves, my children, while I clear up." He began to stack the plates of the meal they had eaten, and Peg led Wheatley downstairs.

"You two," she said over her shoulder, "need your heads banging together."

"Do you think I've offended him?"

"Probably." She went ahead of him across the foyer and opened the library door. "No, probably not. He's as pigheaded about his researches as you are about your poetry." She stopped and turned so suddenly that he was caught by the flurry of her summer skirt. "Sorry, Bob."

"Don't mention it, Peg."

"And you can take that smirk off your face."

"If you stop blushing."

"I'm not. It's the wine. You know it is."

He raised his eyebrows, doubting her, and she put out a hand to hold him at bay. "You do realize

37

what my husband is going on about, don't you? What's on his mind."

"No."

"There's a book missing from the library, and that peculiar little man Gilray has been looking for it. That's what started it all. Fred doesn't believe in ghosts or magic or anything, but he does like to get all his facts stacked up neatly. So the missing book bothers him."

"I thought you kept that sort of thing locked up."

"We do. Of course we do. Nothing's been pinched – not for many, many years, we're quite sure of that."

"So it was lost long ago. What sort of book?"

"A grimoire."

She said nothing else, looking swiftly into his eyes to see if he knew what she meant. He gazed back, and they fenced for a moment, each with a half-smile.

"Well?" she taunted.

"Whose book of spells?" he asked.

"Clever clogs!" She opened the library door.

"You haven't told me," he insisted. "Whose grimoire is it?"

She left him to close the door and walked swiftly away along the library, trailing words behind her. "You've heard of Doctor Carr, I suppose."

"Septimus Carr," he said. "Not that nasty old necromancer again! I might have guessed. The seventh son of a seventh son who thought he could do magic – of course I've heard of him. Who hasn't, hereabouts?"

"What do you know about him?" There was still half the length of the library between them. Their voices echoed.

"Late eighteenth century, early nineteenth," he said. "Lived in Carr Hall, now demolished, out across the fens somewhere towards Littleport. Bit of a rascal."

"More than a bit," she said. "*You* are a bit of a rascal; he was the real thing."

"Doctor Carr chased women, I believe."

"Girls," she said. "Young ones. They were easier."

"Then as now."

"You should know, teacher." She stood in front of the high shelves that Gilray had climbed. "No one who was female was safe from the ghastly doctor."

"He wanted to stay young. Isn't that what the girls were for?"

She nodded. "Fred says he had some idea of eternal life, and that's what his magic was all about. He had to have girls for his wickedness."

"And young, because they had to be virgins. It's old stuff, Peg. Nasty old men always want to rejuvenate themselves with young women." Wheatley took the last few paces to stand in front of her.

"Keep away from me, Bob Wheatley." She pushed him back. "Listen. I must tell you what

39

Mr Gilray told Fred. He said that Septimus Carr carried out awful experiments with the girls."

"There's nothing new in that, Peg. It's a well-known story. Didn't they find a girl dead in the grounds of his house?"

"In the forest. But he wasn't accused; he was too clever."

"Or too powerful. It was very easy for him – the lord of the manor and a servant girl... If he was careful he could have done what he liked in those days."

"Not so different now," she said. "A man has all the advantages."

"Not all."

"Many, especially if the girl is very young." She watched him shrug before she went on. "Septimus Carr had only one use for girls. He believed that the life force, or whatever you care to call it, was even in girls' hair combings, their fingernails, everything to do with them. But it was in fluid mostly, and all fluids carried it, so that's what he really wanted."

"Blood," said Wheatley. "Fresh young blood."

She grimaced. "You disgust me, Bob Wheatley. You must be just like him to be able to even think like that."

"All I have in common with him is that I'm a man, Peg."

"There's a streak in all of you. Men's minds are horrible. But it wasn't only blood with him, he thought the life force was in all fluids."

40

"Oh, Lord," Wheatley groaned, "not that. I suppose he went on about maiden water, like every other foul old magician. W. B. Yeats was just the same... 'Love has pitched his mansion in the place of excrement.'"

"I wouldn't know."

"But you seem to know a terrible lot about the disgusting doctor."

"I've been reading up on it ever since Mr Gilray started to come here. Fred got me interested."

Wheatley looked at her. "I refuse to listen to anyone who wears that expression," he said.

"What expression?"

"Peg," he said, "you're being serious. It's utter nonsense, and you're not laughing at it."

He had hurt her, and in the silence that fell between them he reached for a book that lay on the table. It had a leather spine but it had been damaged and its endboards were missing. "Is this one of the old sorcerer's volumes?" he asked.

She put out a hand and slid the book closer. "This shouldn't be here," she said. "We keep this one locked up with the others."

"Why? What is it?"

"Doctor Carr's diary, and it's already been mauled half to bits. We've had people from all over the place coming to look at this and there's nothing much in it – except it's pretty nasty. But it's all well-known stuff copied from other books about alchemy and magic. There's a lot about clinging on to life for ever and raising the dead."

41

She shuddered. "He seems to have tried some of it."

"And did old Doctor Death ever succeed?"

"What do you think?" She turned a page. "But look at the trouble he took." There was a diagram, and as Wheatley reached out to flatten the thick parchment leaf his hand touched hers. He apologized, and when they bent over the volume he was careful to keep his distance.

The page showed, in spidery outline, a pyramid with tiny human figures drawn at the corners of its base. At the pinnacle, and alongside each figure, or inscribed across its belly, there were signs of the zodiac or what appeared to be chemical formulae.

"Are you sure this isn't the grimoire that's supposed to be missing?" said Wheatley. "That diagram looks very much like a spell to me."

"It's his tomb in the forest," she told him. "And the rest of it is rituals he wanted carried out when he was buried there."

"Spells," said Wheatley.

"Of course." She was curt. Wheatley's attitude was beginning to exasperate her. "These are spells, but nothing unusual. They are all well-known stuff, copied from things like the *Tyrocinium Chymicum* or the *Necrocomicon*." He raised his eyebrows, and she explained for him. "One's a book about alchemy and the *Necrocomicon* is about terrible magic... Mr Gilray wrote down a whole list of books for me. There are lots more."

"Did he hand you the list?" asked Wheatley.

"And did you take it?"

"Of course I did. Why shouldn't I?"

"How did you know he wasn't bewitching you? I'd burn that paper if I were you."

For a moment she took him seriously, but then she saw that he was mocking her, and she coloured. "But you haven't listened to him," she said. "Mr Gilray is convinced that something strange is happening ... that someone is really trying to get in touch with Doctor Carr. And it could be true. There are some funny people about. Maybe he's right to be worried."

"It sounds to me as though you are, too."

"Idiot." She tossed her head. "Oh, I don't know. When you hear him, you almost believe it. He seems to have read everything that's ever been written about old Doctor Damnation, and that's why he came here, because we have all his books."

"Except one."

"Well." She sniffed. "I don't know if that's absolutely true. The missing book is just something that Mr Gilray seems to think should exist. Nobody has ever mentioned such a thing before, according to Fred."

"According to Fred," he repeated, and stared at her until she could hold his eyes no longer, then he turned to the book on the table. "There's one thing I can tell you about this that's far more interesting than anything you've told me yet."

"What's that, Mr Wheatley?"

"Well, just look at it." The pages were so tightly

bound that they each had to press a hand on it to hold it flat. Their heads were close together. "It's very dull," he said. "It hasn't got half the witchcraft that you have in your little finger."

"You can save that line of talk for your cute little schoolgirls, Mr Wheatley, sir. It doesn't work with me."

She turned her head as she spoke and gave a little gasp as if surprised that they should be face to face. But she did not draw back as their lips touched. The book was neglected and, after a while, the page slowly turned itself over until the diagram was hidden.

6

"Lie close," Laura said,
Pricking up her golden head:
"We must not look at goblin men,
We must not buy their fruits:
Who knows upon what soil they fed
Their hungry thirsty roots?"
                    – Christina Rossetti, *Goblin Market*

When Pauline Withers applied for a Saturday job in the bookshop and got it she went straight to Cassandra Ashe and apologized. "You'd be so much better than me," she said. Cassandra looked distressed, and Pauline said hastily, "Perhaps they've made a mistake... I'll give them a ring."

She was turning away, about to do it at once, when her arm was grasped. "You won't do anything so stupid." Cassandra was smiling, but her eyes were moist.

"But you're so disappointed," said Pauline.

"No, I'm not." Cassandra sniffed. It was a

good, loud snuffle but it did not mar her looks in the least. Pauline knew she should have been jealous but she had to struggle not to smile. Cassandra could do anything, and didn't even know how lucky she was. It was unfair. "I'm being stupid," said Cassandra, "but it's your fault. You shouldn't go around saying you're going to give up jobs just because you think someone might be upset."

It was then that Pauline risked saying what was on her mind. "But I thought you wanted to work there because of Nat Woodburn."

"What?" Cassandra's surprise sounded genuine.

"I mean because he works there on Saturdays – and he's very keen on you, Cassandra. Anyone can see that."

"Nat Woodburn?" Cassandra held her at arm's length and examined her face.

Pauline closed her eyes. Was Cassandra blind, or did really beautiful people just not care what effect they had? Anyone else would have noticed at once if Nat Woodburn had even glanced at them. "I thought maybe that's why you wanted the job," she murmured. "I'm sorry."

Cassandra saw the other girl's downturned face and felt the chill of suddenly knowing feelings that were not her own. For an instant she was Pauline, timid and even faintly dowdy. No. No. She trembled, thrusting the thought away, afraid that arrogance would bring bad luck. "I don't want Nat Woodburn," she said.

Suddenly they were holding hands. Cassandra

smiled and Pauline blushed, but it was a pact.

In the bookshop there had been a profound argument over the choice of the Saturday girl. The proprietors had disagreed, but now one of them, Robin Underleaf, was inclined to think that his wife was right. The prettier girl was perhaps less likely to have the purity that the ceremony they had in mind demanded. He looked up from the clumsy little document he was examining.

"I bow to your intuition, dearest heart," he said. "Septimus Carr would doubtless, in life, have preferred the one with the striking looks... "

"Hah!" His wife flung her head back with immense haughtiness. "The short-sightedness of men!"

"... but the little mouse must be our choice."

His wife was immediately magnanimous. "Pray, let me pay tribute once more to your eagle eye. Without you, my sweetest Robin, we should never have had the Master's dying words. Hand me your library pickings, you artful purloiner."

She took from him the small oblong which he held. It was the backboard of a book to which an endpaper was still hinged. Mould had at one time pasted it to the board. "How divinely clever of you to see what mildew had obscured." She glanced briefly at the page, inhaling its odour rather than attempting to read the words scrawled there, then pressed the leaf down until it clung flat to the board. "There – the mould of ages hides it once again." She held it to her forehead. "Dear Master, we shall follow thy wishes to their uttermost end."

Robin Underleaf cleared his throat. "Although the girl Withers may fit the bill," he began.

"Fit the bill! What uncomely phrase is that I hear!"

He began again. "Although Miss Withers may be a suitable offering, nevertheless there is the delicate question of the doctor's elixir, and how we are to obtain it."

"It's perfectly obvious, cretin! We invite the girl to tea."

7

Where Men like Grashoppers appear,
But Grashoppers are Gyants there:
They, in there squeking Laugh, contemn
Us as we walk more low than them.
— Andrew Marvell, *Upon Appleton House*

There was always a hint of dirt, of mildew about Robin Underleaf. His clothes sagged in a tired manner, with an ingrown shabbiness, and he was so short that, seen from behind, he could have been mistaken for a boy, except that he was bald on top.

"Delicious tea," he said. "Quite soul-enhancing, don't you think?"

The question was offered on the prongs of a smile to Pauline Withers, who sat opposite him in the centre of a large sofa. The tea things were on a low table between them.

"It's quite nice," she lied, and sipped at the milkless amber she'd been offered by Mrs Underleaf. It had a nose-wrinkling scent, as raw

49

as geranium leaves, and caught at her throat.

"It's good for you," said Rosa Underleaf. "Good for girls." Her black hair was parted in the middle and drawn back like a ballet dancer's, and she sat as upright as a dancer, holding her cup and saucer with long fingers that were just beginning to gnarl with arthritis. "It has herbs that are particularly good for girls, young girls particularly. It delays the degenerative process. How old do you think I am?"

The black curves of her raised eyebrows were matched by the faintly purple sag of the wrinkles beneath, and the question swam in the tiredness of her huge, dark eyes.

"I don't know," said Pauline shyly. "Not very old, I shouldn't think."

"Shouldn't think!" The echo was shrill. "I am charmed: 'Not *very* old, I shouldn't think!'" Rosa Underleaf made a balletic gesture with one slender hand as if she were casting flowers upon the air, and laughed. "How honest, how sweetly honest of you, Pauline my dear."

"I only meant..." said Pauline.

"Yes?" The head jutted forward to present the large eyes as two tender receptacles bravely ready to absorb the painful fact, no matter what, that was about to be plunged into them.

"I only meant how young you look, Rosa." Using Mrs Underleaf's first name was still strange to her, and she shyly lowered her eyes.

"Doesn't she look sweet when she does that?"

Rosa, again as vertical as a lighthouse, turned to her husband. "And very, very young. No more than a child."

He had his teacup on his knees, held by both hands, and was crouched over it, sniffing its vapours like a dog. "Both of you, my dear wife. Both of you very young indeed."

"Enough!" A hand scythed the air in a graceful gesture of contempt. "Enough of this flattery, and to business. Drink up, Pauline, drink."

Pauline could not refuse. She drained her cup and watched uneasily as it was refilled. Having tea with Robin and Rosa Underleaf had always been a daunting prospect, but she had not had the courage to say no to her employers. And now she was in the big room that overlooked a broad, tree-lined avenue, and she was dizzy with shyness.

"To business?" Robin Underleaf was crouched so low in his deep armchair that Pauline saw that the fringe of long hair at the back of his head was spread out across his shoulders, and she felt sorry for him. He could not enjoy being so short and bald, and being married to Rosa must be an ordeal. He smiled at Pauline rather sweetly, and she managed to smile back. "I wonder what business my lady wife can be referring to?"

"The man's grotesque," said Rosa. Surely she was referring to his opinions and not his looks, but it was a cruel slip of the tongue. Pauline was gazing down into her lap when Rosa thrust aside any doubt as to what she meant. "Just look at him!

Snuffling over his tea like a hideous little poodle."

Full of compassion for him, Pauline raised her eyes. But Rosa was cruelly accurate. Robin Underleaf was panting, showing his tongue.

"He enjoys being insulted," said his wife. "I think that's the most revolting thing about him."

Pauline had no answer but had to do something. "Excuse me." She put her cup on the table. "I must go upstairs."

"What on earth for?" Rosa's eyes were closed.

"Well..." said Pauline, praying that she would be understood.

"The loo is out of order." Rosa turned away. "Now look here, Robin Underleaf, are you or are you not a man of your word?"

"What word is that, my love?" He had straightened in his chair.

"Ghost," she said.

The room had become quiet. It seemed to Pauline that its size had increased. Everything had shifted out of her reach. The decorated plasterwork of the ceiling was a canopy of pale leaves far overhead, and the real leaves of the conservatory that showed through the window at the back of the room held a shallow, distant sunlight. The other window looked beyond the slope of the long front garden to the avenue and the park beyond it from which came the far away shouts of boys' laughter and a girl's squeal. She had never felt so alone.

"Ghost." Robin Underleaf stood up. "It's one of my sillier ideas, isn't that so, my dearest helpmeet?" He was barely taller than his sitting wife. She did not deign to reply. "I am by way of being a student of the occult, of matters extraordinary."

"For heaven's sake get on with it!" Rosa sighed deeply and put the back of her hand to her brow. "We are impatient."

He sniggered. "She thinks me a fool." He paused as if waiting for her to deny it, but she was silent and he had to continue. "However, I have come across an account of a spectral presence somewhere hereabouts which will manifest itself only in the presence of a pure young maiden, and I wish…"

"Oh, for God's sake!" Rosa leant suddenly towards Pauline. "The idiot wants to know if you are a virgin. Are you?"

Pauline sat rigidly still, hearing the blood sing its thin song in her ears.

"She is," said Rosa. "That's obvious. But whether she will assist you in your utterly ridiculous attempt to snare a poltergeist I very much doubt. Pauline, my sweet young thing, what is the trouble?"

Pauline was on her feet. "Excuse me," she said. "But I must go."

"See what you have done to her, you odious male. You have terrified her and she wishes to leave."

"No." Pauline's heart pounded. "It's not that. It's all that tea. I've really got to go."

"Oh, that." Rosa was quite unruffled. "Upstairs, my dear." She waved a hand, directing her to the door.

"But you said…"

"Our room … our bedroom, you'll find what you require."

Pauline, gone pale, left the room. They heard her begin to climb the stairs.

"Poor child," said Rosa Underleaf to her husband, "I notice that you do not react to her as you did to the superficial prettiness of the other one."

"Perhaps not," he said, "but she'll do. She'll do very well."

"As you say, my pet."

They listened until they heard their bedroom door close, and then they smiled pleasantly at each other.

8

A tremor circled through the gloom,
*   As if a crash upon the floor*
Had jarred and shaken all the room:
*   For nearly all the listening things*
Were old and worn, and knew what curse
*   Of violent change death often brings,*
From good to bad, from bad to worse
                    – James Thomson ("B.V."), *In the Room*

Linda Blake, in the faint light from the dashboard, looked sideways at Gary Prentice and said, "I don't blame her, really."

"Who?"

"My mother. I think she quite fancies you."

He laughed. "Well, as a matter of fact..."

She dug her fingernails into his arm. "If you do so much as smile at her, I'll..."

"You'll what, sweetheart?"

"Well," she lay back, "I just might tell my father."

"Tell Daddy." He was sneering. "Tell Daddy and he'll give me the sack – that it?"

"I can't help it if he's your boss. And don't call me sweetheart, you oik."

He was amused. "You're a right little bitch," he said. "I go for your mother every time."

She could just make out his blunt profile, snub nose and eyebrows bunched in a frown as he concentrated on the road ahead. She guessed his eyesight was not good, but he would never admit it. "You want to know something?"

"What?"

"I think you'd look great in glasses." His heavy chin went up a fraction. "You'd be sort of tough but intellectual. But don't do it just because I say so, because you'd make all the girls go mad – except my mother, that is. She goes for the oily sweatshirt and black fingernail brigade."

"Pity your old man promoted me, then. I always liked it when your mother come shimmying in and I was lying under a motor."

"You randy, deceitful, sex-obsessed yob. No wonder you're a used car salesman."

"That's where you're wrong, darlin'. We don't deal in old tat at Paragon bloody Motors."

"Used cars. That's where you belong, because that's what you are."

"If you wasn't just a kid I'd open the door and give you the heave."

"Don't call me kid."

"Ain't you still at school, then?"

"What does that matter?" Linda Blake enjoyed quarrelling with him. "Can I help it if I prefer older men? And I don't mean overgrown schoolboys like you – I mean mature men. There's someone I know who's particularly nice."

"Who's that, then?"

It was not an idle question; he wanted to know. He was jealous, and she played on it. "He's a teacher – and he's really yummy. He isn't into all that sex stuff like you. It's all poetry with him and he really gives you the shivers with it."

"They teach you some crap at that school, then."

"How would you know? He could have any girl he wants – but he's nice, not like you at all."

"Don't you believe it, darlin'. He ain't no different. What, with all them sixth form girls? – just give him half a chance." Gary gave a grunt and a hoo-hoo-hoo like an ape.

"You're disgusting, did you know that?" But she was not displeased, and he knew it.

"Well, you shouldn't be here in the same cage as me, should you, darlin'?"

She was silent. They always had played the game of threats, so there was no danger from him, but she suddenly hated the way he called her darling. He'd say it to any woman, just as he'd call any man mate. It made her one of the herd, the females. "Darlin'!" she said contemptuously. "I'm not your darlin' at all."

"I'm the best you're likely to get."

57

"Conceit! The vanity of the man!" One day, however, she would so humiliate him that he would say darling to her and mean it. The thought made her wriggle in her seat.

"What would old buggerlugs think about you and me, then?" he asked.

"My dad's got nothing to do with it."

"I never meant your father." He sensed he was on dangerous ground with her, and hastily corrected the idea in her mind. "I was talking about that teacher you was going on about."

"I wasn't going on about him – I just said that Mr Wheatley was quite nice for a teacher."

"Him!" Gary, recognizing the man, yelped with laughter. "He thinks he's something, but he don't know his arse from his elbow. I used to do his motor for him – if you can call that clapped out banger a set of wheels."

"Well, anyway." Enough had been said about Gary's passion for motors. "He hasn't got much time for cars," she said. "He likes to bike."

"Old Bob Wheatley." Gary was loving it. "I see him every day, practically, on that bloody old pushbike weighted down with books. I should think you Richards are quite safe with him."

"Richards?"

"Richard the Thirds – birds."

She laughed. "That's insulting – like everything you say."

"It turns *you* on, though, don't it? – a bit of aggro."

She leant forward and gazed upward through the windscreen. They were driving through a channel of black trees which intensified the thick porridge of stars overhead. Bob Wheatley was still in her mind and suddenly she found herself saying, "'Look at the stars! look, look up at the skies! O look at all the fire-folk sitting in the air!'"

"What you on about now?"

"Nothing much," she said. "Only that loving someone is nice."

"It sounded like a load of crap about stars to me."

"Poem," she said. "Words."

He was laughing, shaking his head. "You kill me," he said.

She leant back so that she could see the shape of his close-cropped, round head. "It would take more than a girl to kill you, Gary Prentice. You look pretty strong."

That pleased him. "I may be strong, but I ain't all that pretty."

But she knew he believed he was good-looking; the cloud of aftershave around him made it too obvious. Suddenly, hating herself for knowing too much, she pressed close to him and kissed his neck. He was so clean that the oils he used on himself completely erased any smell of the man. "Want to know something?" she asked.

"What?"

"I'm scared."

"There's nothing to worry about, darlin'."

There was a gap in the verge where a track led through the trees. He pulled off the road, stopped and switched off. "I'll look after you," he said.

"That's what I'm scared of. I think I'm going to shiver. I didn't expect it to be so dark."

He reached to the back seat, lifted a can and pulled the ring. "Try this," he said. "You'll feel braver."

Gary was everything he should be. It was lager. It tasted cold and metallic, and she didn't like it. "But we've got to go a long way before we come to the tomb," she said. "What if we get lost again?"

"We almost made it last night. I been looking at the map. Or we'll get the old sod to come out of his bloody grave and fetch us to him."

"Don't say that." She hunched her shoulders. "You said he killed a girl, don't forget."

"About two hundred years ago. Not yesterday."

"But that's what he did, and you said he was cruel to girls anyway. And that's why you want me with you, isn't it? – because you have this crazy idea I might tempt his ghost to come out."

"He ain't the only one who likes to have a bit of crumpet around."

"You're sick!" But she was laughing as she fended him off, slid out of the car and ran away among the trees.

By the time he had caught up with her they were deep within the forest, and although she struggled she was glad to be in the circle of his arms. There

60

was a sterile stillness around them, without light or sound or air.

His mouth found hers. "Ghost bait," he said.

"Don't say that." For answer he kissed her again, and she said, "You don't really believe all this ghost stuff, do you, Gary?"

He took his arms from around her but held her hand. "I feel lucky," he whispered, and she went with him deeper into the darkness.

She knew, well before he had realized it, that they had reached the place. The trees were spaced so that the stars were visible, and in what light filtered down from the sky she saw the pyramid. When she held back, he saw it, too.

"Spot on!" He kept his voice low, but the sound still made her shiver. "I bloody knew it!"

"I heard something!"

They listened. Not even a grass blade stirred. "There's nobody here but us chickens."

"But there was last night." She held back. "I told you I saw something."

"A bloody old owl," he said. "We both heard it."

But there had been something else, a dark shape high in the trees and bigger than an owl, much bigger. "It wasn't an owl," she said and tried to draw back, but they had passed the moment when it might have been possible.

He put his arm around her and suddenly charged towards the pyramid. "If you're there," he shouted, "come and see what I've got for you!"

"Don't!" She tried to turn back, but he forced her forward.

"Don't go and spoil everything," he said. "You know it's only a bit of fun."

"No it isn't." She wrenched herself free, and they stood facing each other in the clearing. Her fear dwindled. She felt ridiculous. "It's not funny any more," she said. "It's gone too far. You've hurt my arm."

He let out his breath. "Trust a bint to bugger it up." He snatched at her wrist and began to tug her around the tomb. "I ain't come this far for nothing."

She pleaded with him to let go, but he shouted into the darkness, "I got a girl! Come and get her, if you can!"

At the door he battered on the iron. "Open up, you old sod – I got a woman for ya!"

She was sobbing now, struggling to free herself, but Gary had too much muscle. He drew her towards the window opening in the pyramid's sloping side.

"Spook!" he shouted, and his voice echoed within the black chamber. "Old spook, I got someone who wants to meet ya!"

"Stop it." She was gasping like a swimmer too far from land. "Please, Gary, I don't want any more of this."

"You was keen enough to start it." He listened at the opening but heard nothing. "Not a bloody squeak. Perhaps he only shows hisself to virgins.

If you are a virgin."

She said nothing.

He put his head close to the opening. "She won't tell me, mister," he said. "You better come and find out for yourself." He breathed in deeply, and turned to face her. "You won't believe this, darlin', but I can smell the old devil. Do you want a sniff?"

She pulled back.

"He ain't sure whether you're a virgin or not, and I ain't either, so I reckon I got to find out." He laughed. "Don't go away and leave me, will ya?" His thick fingers tightened on her wrist. "I'll just get rid of me booze first." He drank, then pushed his empty can through the bars. "That's for you, old 'un."

Linda heard him grunt. Something puzzled him. "What?" he said, and then, his voice rising a step each time he repeated it, he said again and again, "Wha'? Wha'? Wha'?" And suddenly, using all his force, he lunged backwards. "Somethin' held me!" he yelled. "There's some bloody thing in there! It held me!"

He put out his hand. Even in the lack of light they could both see dark streaks from his knuckle to his wrist.

"That's blood. I'm bloody bleeding! It got its bloody fangs into me!"

"No." She tried to calm him. "You caught it on the wire."

"It clawed me, I tell ya!"

"There's nothing there, Gary."

"What do you know about it? What the bloody hell do you bloody know?"

"You imagined it, Gary."

"You callin' me a coward, are ya?" He came towards her and she backed away. "Are ya?" She shook her head but it was not enough. "Jesus Christ, she's callin' me a coward!"

"No."

He loomed over her. "That's your word, in't it? The only soddin' word you know – No! No! No!" As his voice rose his fist went up, and at the final scream he brought it down. Then, as each blow added satisfaction to the lovely heat of his rage, he struck again and again.

Linda sagged at the jar of the first blow, but then rode on the shock of the second as if it had happened at a great distance. By the time his fist hit her for the third time she was a tiny speck disappearing into a tightening whirlpool of infinite pain. The fourth punch, which he delivered kneeling over her, could not reach where she had gone.

9

Bards of Passion and of Mirth,
Ye have left your souls on earth!
— John Keats, "Ode"

When the rest of the class filed out through the lobby at the end of the classroom and clattered down the steps into the school grounds, Cassandra Ashe, who had followed them to the door, hung back. She was sure Mr Wheatley would listen to her, but she was nervous. Even more so because he had failed to notice her at the back of the room and thought he was alone.

He scratched his groin. She bit her lip. Then he moved to the window near his desk, raised his arms high over his head as he stretched and looked out into the trees. He began to bend forward.

"Sir," she said in a half-voice so as to be both heard and not heard simultaneously.

"Christ!" He found himself spinning around,

arms still above his head. It was, he realized, a goddamned pirouette.

"Oh!" she said.

"Ah." He let out his breath, but could not think of a plausible way out of his ballet dancer's pose so kept his arms high. His ankles were crossed. He gritted his teeth.

"I wanted to see you, Mr Wheatley."

"Uh-huh." He stretched higher, pretending to yawn, but he stumbled as he began to lower his hands and uncross his legs. He groaned.

"Have you strained something, Mr Wheatley?"

"Only my self-esteem." He straightened. "I was just…" he waved an arm as he began to explain, then gave up. "Never mind." She had advanced, clutching a pile of books, and he recognized them as his own. "You've finished with them, have you?"

"Oh no, not yet. I'm still enjoying them." She pressed them to her bosom.

"Lucky poets." Hang back, Wheatley. This is a girl. You can't trade innuendos with girls as you can with boys. Especially one with a mouth like a rosy O. Be detached; your mission, Wheatley, should you accept it, is to listen to what those lips are saying.

He raised one eyebrow, and she quaked. He's never, she thought, done that before; not to me. "Sir," she said, "I don't know what to do."

"No?" He smiled and saw her gaze quiver. Take care, Wheatley. Impressionable sixteen. "It won't do," he said aloud, addressing himself.

"What won't, Mr Wheatley?"

"All those volumes of verse I have thrust your way, Cassandra. That's what won't do. The words boxed there are like a murmur of travelling bees. They are subversive. They will sting you to death." He had said too much.

"I know, Mr Wheatley. That's what I like."

Their eyes met and, for one instant, like blades touching, sparked. Then her lids drooped. "But I wasn't talking about that," she said. "It's Linda Blake. She's missing."

"Run off with someone, I understand." He was the teacher again, a brisk know-all.

"Two days ago."

"And you know where they are – is that what's worrying you?"

She shook her head.

"Well, do you know *him* – the young man?"

"Not really." She came forward until she was pressing against the desk. "But I know where they were going that night." She told him about the meeting in the forest, and saw him smile.

"I should think they're a long way from there by now, Cassandra. The police say so."

She was alarmed. "The police?"

"They've questioned every member of staff," he said. "It was all very discreet. They think it was planned some time ago, false trails and everything. So it doesn't look as if she told you the truth."

"But she did! I know she did!"

Her sudden vehemence surprised him. "None of this is your fault, Cassandra. You know what sort of girl she was."

"Was?"

"Is." He drew in his breath. Too much teenage drama was creeping in. "Nothing has happened to her," he said. "Nothing she didn't plan. If I know anything about Linda Blake she's leading some young guy a merry dance somewhere."

"Gary Prentice," said Cassandra.

"So you *do* know him."

"Just that he worked for her father."

Wheatley nodded. The staffroom knew. Her father owned the largest garage in town. "Well, it's up to the police what happens next. I don't see that we can do anything."

She watched him take his jacket from the back of the chair and begin to put it on. He was smug. He didn't understand. Her voice was sulky, disappointed. "There's the pyramid," she said.

She saw him hesitate. For a moment he did not seem to know what she meant, but then he looked at her from the corner of his eye. The pyramid. So he did know about it. "Gary was going to take her there to try to find a ghost," she said. He frowned, and she added quickly, "I know you won't believe any of this, Mr Wheatley – and I don't, either, but Gary was funny like that. He had books."

They had walked the length of the room as they talked. "You don't have to pay too much attention to people like Gary Prentice," he said.

68

"But what if something happened there?"

"Such as?"

Exasperated, she shook her head. "Oh, I don't know, do I! I just thought someone ought to go out there and see." She could not face him. "And I daren't go to the police – they'd just think I was getting worked up about nothing. You know what they're like."

"I haven't had that pleasure."

Her eyes flicked up and caught his smile. He had become commonplace. Unheroic. She turned away and went through the door.

"I see I have disappointed you, Miss Ashe."

The voice at her back made her pause inside the narrow lobby that served as a cloakroom. She heard him come in behind her.

"You forget I am just a bloodless bloody teacher. Keeping my nose clean."

A single forgotten winter coat hung on the row of hooks inside the lobby, and the air smelt of old shoes. She turned. "Would you take me there?"

"Would I what?"

"Go there with me."

"You certainly know how to spring a surprise, Cassandra. Why me?"

"There's no one else." She regarded the knot of his tie. "No one I can trust. My father won't have anything to do with it ... and he says I shouldn't, either."

"Your father is right."

Without hurry, standing close to him, she

lowered her eyelids then raised them slowly. The lobby was as warm as a beehive, musty. It was a dangerous scent, and the pulse of herself that she had released by the veiling and unveiling of her eyes clamoured louder there than the murmur of any bees. "Please, Mr Wheatley."

In the flat above the museum Peg Wherry asked Gilray how he liked his coffee.

"Three sugary-wugaries this morning," he said.

She looked down on him as he sat at the table, still wearing his raglan coat and porkpie hat, and still with the distracted, worried expression on his face that had made her take pity on him. She put three heaped spoons into the cup on the table in front of him. "Demerara," she said. "OK?"

He sipped without stirring, then looked up with his snaggle-toothed grin. "Is prime, my sweetheart. Is prime."

In order not to laugh she handed him a packet of Jaffa cakes and said, "Bicky?" It was catching.

He took a biscuit and examined it. "Is something new?" he asked.

"Hardly."

"Chocky base," he observed, and bit it. "And orangy middledy-diddle!"

Then her laughter had to come. "Have you never seen a Jaffa cake!" she said. "Where on earth do you come from?"

"Where indeed." He was laughing with her when he suddenly noticed he was still wearing his hat. "Oh, please excuse titfer, hospitable madam." He placed it on the table.

She watched him smooth the few strands of hair across his damp scalp, and her pity returned. She had found him in the library moaning with distress because he had been unable to find any of the papers relating to the pyramid tomb. "I'm sorry that Fred won't be back till tonight," she said. "He's in Cambridge all day, and I didn't even know he'd taken all that stuff with him."

"I am in deep, deep puzzlement," said Gilray. "His meeting is to do with money?"

"Yes," she said. "He's applying for a local history research grant from the Arts Board. It's nothing to do with the Doctor Carr thing, but you know what Fred's like when he gets his teeth into something – I expect he thought there might be someone at the Fitzwilliam who could help him while he's in Cambridge."

It was no consolation to Gilray. "Cambridge is miles and miles and miles," he whimpered, "and I have only my bike."

"Is it really that urgent, Mr Gilray?"

"Oh, lady," he said, and there was genuine anguish in the face he turned towards her. "A girl may be in danger!"

Nat Woodburn skived off early. It was a sixth former's privilege, but he overdid it in order to show that he placed no value on it.

It was mid-morning when he sauntered slowly

past the head's window in order to be seen on his way to the gate. Strange how the cold sweat broke out on the sides of his chest, not exactly in the armpits, although he raised his elbows just in case oval damp patches were forming, visual and olfactory proof of cowardice. I'm walking like a pregnant penguin, he thought, and flapped his arms slowly.

"You OK, Woodburn?"

The voice made him jump and twist his head. "Oh, it's you, sir." Bob Wheatley had come out of a side door. "I thought it was someone in authority."

"Watch it, Woodburn. I've got the goods on you. What time do you call this?"

"Time to forgive and forget, sir. My aunt has suffered a severe thrombosis and is not expected to last the hour. I'm dashing to her bedside."

"Where does she live?"

"Newcastle-on-Tyne, sir." He realized that Wheatley was looking at his raised elbows. "I intend to fly, sir. Time is pressing."

"One last question, Woodburn."

"Yes, sir?"

"Who is she?"

"Mrs Mabel Cockburn, sir – pronounced cock, after her husband, who is a very prominent citizen."

"Cease! you prurient romancer. I do not refer to your non-existent relative, I am asking who's the girl in the case?"

"In the *shop*, sir. It's a lady in a shop."

"The truth at last. Your pasty face and sunken eye betray you, Woodburn." Wheatley began to move away. "You're a girlstruck moron."

"It takes one to know one," said Nat, sliding through the gateway, "sir."

10

Wonderful things
                    – Howard Carter

The Market Place, tinned over with parked cars, glittered in Nat's mind like a magic lake. An old dosser, who staked a claim to every cranny of occupiable space in the centre of town, stood at the entrance to the alleyway by The Ship. Lance Hunt, padded with the armour of many coats, shuffled into Nat's path.

"Hail, Sir Lancelot," said Nat.

"Bollocks." Lance had a huge body composting within the dun layers he wore, and a fist the size of a sugar beet.

Knowing what was needed, Nat held out a coin. The beet turned over, unclenched its roots, then closed over the piece of silver Nat dropped into it.

Lance touched the mouldering peak of the cap that was pulled far down over the shining red

74

stubble of his face. "Thanks, mate, you mean bugger," he said.

The alleyway joined others, and behind The Ship there was a small, dark crossroads where a little shop's crooked windows managed to command all four directions at once. It was Dickens and Disneyland, and Nat approached it like a dwarf entering a diamond mine. The proprietor greeted him as the doorbell jangled.

"How frightfully brave!" Rosa Underleaf was trembling with admiration. "I watched that brutish animal accost you and I feared for your safety, I really did! Yet you stood and *reasoned* with him and didn't turn a hair. What on earth did you find to say to him?"

Nat shrugged. "I made a small donation towards his overheads, and he thanked me effusively."

Both hands flew to Rosa's mouth. "His overheads!" Even the bookshelves that pressed in from all sides did not prevent her laughter ringing out. "Lance Hunt's overheads! I can't wait to tell hubby."

At the back of the shop the office was no more than a cubbyhole curtained off. Rosa's perfume mingled with the scent of old books, and she intensified it by drawing the curtain closed behind Nat and herself. Still standing, she angled her head to look sideways at him.

"I don't know if I should do this," her vividly red lips turned down in doubt, "but what the hell!"

She waved her long and slightly crooked fingers to a wooden chair squeezed into a corner and he sat himself down while she manoeuvred herself behind the ancient desk that took up most of the floor space. Two was a crowd in here.

"Let me see." She raised both hands level with her shoulders and spread them outwards, at the same time gazing at the floor behind the desk. "What is it you men prefer at this time of day?"

"I hardly like to say," said Nat.

The lids of her enormous eyes trembled and she shifted slightly, smiling secretively as she continued to peer beneath the desk. "You have always looked like a beer man to me," and she reached down and lifted a bottle from the floor. "It has to be a bottle, I'm afraid. Hubby is an appalling wimp about that; he doesn't approve of people drinking from cans."

"Civilized," said Nat, and accepted a glass and an opener with the bottle. "But aren't you drinking with me?"

"Wicked boy! What would that ogre say if he caught us *boozing* together?" She closed her eyes, but the smile lingered. "I'll have a teentsy sherry."

She turned to a library cabinet behind her. "We call this the Port and Pornography Department," she said as she unlocked the door and took out a decanter and sherry glass. "Hubby keeps disgusting things in there."

"The secret sediment of his soul," said Nat, then felt uncomfortable as she fixed him with eyes so solemn they seemed to accuse him of impertinence.

He struggled and came out with, "Everyone has a secret cupboard ..." the stare did not vary "... somewhere."

Holding her glass between finger and thumb, with three fingers extended, she took a minute sip, put her glass down, and in a sudden flare of mischief said, "I wonder what you have hidden away in your secret cupboard, Nathaniel. Wonderful things?"

They were the words Howard Carter had used when he first glimpsed through a crack what lay within Tutankhamen's tomb. Wonderful things. Did she know? What was in her mind? Before he had a chance to speak, she was off on another tack.

"Were you wondering why I asked you to drop in for this little tête-à-tête? It's because we are very pleased with you." She turned her head suddenly and spoke to herself in disgust. "Pleased with him! How frightfully like an employer you sound, Rosa Underleaf!"

"I don't mind."

"Sweet!" She faced him. "You *are* a plum-cake, aren't you? And I can tell you are practically pleading with me to beg a favour from you."

"Of course I am," he said, and added, "Rosa."

Shyly, her eyelids fluttered. "Dear boy," she said, "we would like you to spend a full day here on your own. In charge."

Her attitude had led him to expect something more exciting; he had already been in charge at lunchtimes while both Rosa and her husband were away. "If you think I'm up to it," he said.

"Darling!" She reached across the desk and clutched his hand. "Robin and I would be ecstatically grateful. It is eons since we have had a weekend entirely to ourselves."

"Any time that suits you," he said.

"Saturday." She released her hand and sat back. "Of course, there are inducements."

He made a moue and shrugged.

"So disdainful!" She was filled with admiration. "You must know how attractive that is to women, you shameless male."

"I wouldn't say that."

"How impetuously modest! You are becoming so ridiculously irresistible that I begin to doubt I should inform you of the inducement I was to offer." She became coy. "It's female."

He did not dare meet her eyes.

She paused, deliberately stirring his interest. "You know we have been looking for a new young lady to help us out – Well, we have found one, and she is to be with you."

Cassandra Ashe. He knew she had applied. He was suddenly disgusted with himself for having felt pleasure when Rosa had pressed his hand.

"I gather she is rather keen on a certain young gentleman of her own age, so she is very eager to work alongside him on Saturday."

"Oh, yes?" He was nonchalant, but the blood sang in his ears.

"Pauline Withers," said Rosa.

Nat Woodburn drank his beer. It had no flavour.

"She's so sweet, so shy."

He nodded.

"Darling," said Rosa, "you will be kind to her, won't you?"

He did not have to answer. The doorbell jangled, and footsteps sounded on the other side of the curtain. They scuffled a little but were too purposeful to be those of a customer. Rosa had lifted her glass and was drinking when the curtain was pushed aside and Robin Underleaf's sharp countenance was thrust through, the head alone, like Mr Punch.

"Just look at him," she laughed gaily. "He's as suspicious as a weasel!"

Robin Underleaf smiled.

"All pointed teeth and menace, isn't he? And what is that he is carrying? – something revolting, I'll be bound."

Her husband pushed the curtain further aside and came into the cubicle. There was not enough room for him, but he squeezed behind her seat to stand in front of the cabinet. As he fished for his keys she said, "It's open." He had placed a small bottle with a glass stopper on the desk in front of her. She very carefully refrained from touching it, but asked, "What is this, pray?"

He glanced suspiciously over his shoulder at Nat, snatched it up and locked it away.

"Charming!" she cried. "Nathaniel, I free you from your promise – we shall not be requiring you.

Our weekend shall not take place!"

Mystified, Robin Underleaf gave a snuffling little giggle.

"You are rude, you are secretive, you are abominable. I refuse to have anything more to do with you until you tell the young man what is in the bottle!"

"Only something for my hobby, dearest heart."

"Which is?" She turned the blaze of her eyes on Nat as she awaited her husband's answer.

"Ghost-hunting, my love."

"And the bottle?"

"It is an inducement to the ghost to come forth."

"Cretin!" She laughed with abandon. "Which ghost? Where?"

"I'd rather not say, my love." He did not look at her.

She leant forward to focus her attention entirely on Nat. "As a clergyman's son, Nathaniel, what is your opinion of the paltry pursuits of my spouse?"

"At least it's not stamp-collecting."

"Ha! So you are a man too! Not a word of criticism to another male. The clan gathers, and I, a mere female, am outnumbered."

"I wouldn't say you were mere."

"Well, well, how sweet you can be when you try." She beamed on him, and heaved a bosom-befriending sigh. "I suppose, when all is said and done, boys will be boys, and we women must indulge you. Have your little secrets together whenever you will. I shall not interfere." She raised her glass. "Down the hatch – is that what you say to one another? Bottoms up, my old cock sparrow!"

Robin Underleaf whinnied and looked slyly at Nat. Nat lowered his eyes.

11

A savage place! as holy and enchanted
As e'er beneath a waning moon was haunted
By woman wailing for her demon lover!
                    – S. T. Coleridge, *Kubla Khan*

The car rattled at every bump. "It's coins," said Bob Wheatley. "They get under the floorboards."

Cassandra was uncertain. "Floorboards in a car?" she asked.

"That's a point." He thought for a moment. "It must be something working loose. I've been wondering why I could see the road through there." He pointed to the base of the gear stick, and there was a hole through which she could see the tarmac streaming by. "No trouble in this weather," he said, "but it gets draughty in winter."

She looked to see if he was joking but he was placidly facing ahead. "It's a nice car, anyway," she lied.

"I've seen better," he said. He heard her snuffle

and glanced anxiously towards her. "Dammit, Cassandra, you're laughing at me."

"I can't help it," she said, and the laughter came. "You don't know anything about cars, do you?"

"I understand bikes." He was ruefully amused. "More or less."

All her nervousness at being with him was washed away in the laughter she could not stop. "You're hopeless!" She leant forward to try to get her breath, and saw the hole in the floor. It was his air conditioning. She shook and ached.

Wheatley, not in the joke, smiled. He glanced at her as she rubbed her tears away, and a picture of himself was suddenly sharp in his mind. The mottled mirror on his wardrobe door, and himself looking into it as he put on a clean shirt getting ready to go out. To meet a schoolgirl. He winced, as he had done less than an hour ago. He had caught sight of himself dressing as if to go out on a date. With a schoolgirl. The blotched image had been suddenly too accurate and he had let his tie fall to the floor and resumed the shirt he had worn all day. Relief made him sigh again. She was, after all, quite safe with him.

"I'm sorry, Mr Wheatley," she said. "I couldn't help it."

"Don't worry about it, Cassandra." He had enjoyed seeing her laugh.

They came to the forest and he had to ask her where they should stop. The road ran in a bright groove through the colonnades of trees where the dusk was already being induced, and she also was unsure. He caught sight of a picket marking a fire break and he swung into the opening and got out of the car. "This'll do as well as anywhere," he said, the teacher once more. "Let's go."

Wherever a patch of sunlight showed among the trees purple fireweed grew shoulder height, and a long tongue of the tall flowers marked the track and penetrated the forest. It was a place for lovers, but Wheatley and his pupil each kept to a separate tractor rut.

After a while he looked back. The car was out of sight. The woods around them were silent. "And no birds sing," he said. "Have you noticed?"

The rows of conifers sprang up as rank as ferns from the forest floor, and the thought of the pyramid made her anxious. "We've got to find it and get out of here," she said.

"I know how you feel. It's just like being Peter Rabbit in Mr McGregor's garden ... or is that too childish for you?"

"A bit bookish, sir."

He apologized.

She wanted to let her hand trail through the purple flowers, but that would have been too girlish and coy. It may even make him apologize again. Oh, damn. "I think it's that way," she said.

They had come to a place where two tracks crossed, and she pointed along one that was densely overgrown. Linda Blake had told her that the pyramid was away from where the trees grew in straight rows, in an older, neglected part of forest. "We could try."

"Right." Wheatley wanted to act quickly, get it over with. He went ahead, making a channel for her through the long grass. He was pleased to have his back to her, to be in charge and thrusting ahead carelessly.

She saw the slope of muscle through his shirt and for a moment he ceased to be a teacher. Then she killed the thought.

Wheatley was the first to spot the tomb. "My God," he said, "it exists!"

Beneath Gilray's feet the spongy bed of pine needles was distasteful. Walking on it made his limbs ache, but it was necessary to search the tomb by daylight and he did not wish to risk flying and be seen. Besides, flying took even more effort than walking and he needed to ration his energies. He undid the buttons of his raglan.

"A little flapjack of air may bring easement," he said and fanned the forest odours with the wings of his coat. It brought little comfort, however, and he stood still, resting.

Cassandra stood beside Wheatley at the edge of the clearing. Dank weeds pressed close to the tomb.

"It's as ugly as a Methodist chapel," he said. Its grey sides were unevenly crusted with lichen, and the columns at the entrance were squat and unimpressive. It was a collection of clichés, and he added another. "Abandon hope," he said, "all ye who enter here." He banged the flat of his hand against the iron door, but it was too solid to resound. "Come out, old ghost!" he called. "Tell us what happened here."

"Don't," she said. "Please don't, Mr Wheatley."

He turned towards her and saw that she was serious. Anger at the silly, solemn girl made him abrupt. "Why not?"

"It doesn't seem right." She looked away, knowing that he found her foolish. "I'm sure something happened to Linda. And she did come here – she said so."

Her seriousness had become mawkishly adult and self-dramatizing, as if she was yearning for a tragedy so that she could shed lovely tears. He welcomed the fact that she had become unattractive, and he swung away from her and began to circle the tomb.

He discovered the window slot cut into its side and was puzzled by it. It began at ground level and was protected by a metal grille, but instead of glass behind the metal bars there was a rusted wire mesh. He leant closer and saw that the pyramid was only the outer shape of the mausoleum and the slot was a window to admit light to the space inside. The pyramid contained a single room, a hollow cube, and he could see, on the far side, another barred opening through which the forest was visible.

There was a tombstone in the floor, in the centre, and the walls were painted. There were robed figures, including a pretty enough, if pallid, girl in some sort of clinging garment, and symbols of day and night, a crescent moon, a gilded sunburst, and others less easy to identify. It had a spurious antiquity, but its feebleness was blurred by the flaking paint and a hint of the grandeur of true aging.

He drew back, displeased with himself for being even faintly awed. "Smells like a public lavatory," he said.

Cassandra hated him for diminishing it, and turned her back. "I'm going right round," she told him.

He followed. How ordinary her blonde hair, how solid her footsteps. And how stupid of him to have ever believed that this girl, a mere parcel of puerile prejudices, could have ever been desirable, a danger. They came back to where they had started.

"There's not a thing," he said caustically. "No body, no bloodstains, nothing at all satisfying."

She had taken her turn to gaze through the bars. "There's a beer can in there," she said.

"Well, what would you expect?" The whole thing was an invitation to the credulous to bring their offerings. A lager can was no more than it deserved.

"Will you reach it for me, Mr Wheatley?"

"What on earth for?"

She did not answer but stood in front of him, an uncertain schoolgirl, even swinging her skirt and unable to meet his eyes. Perhaps she thought the can was some sort of evidence, and he took a grudging pity on her. He had taken a foolish risk to bring her here, a teacher and a schoolgirl in the woods together. But to reach for the beer can would be to do her a favour, a small bribe. He smiled at her, playing the part of an indulgent adult. "You're a funny girl," he said, and he crouched to put his arm through a hole that someone had punched in the wire mesh.

The can was at the limit of his reach and he had to use his fingertips to walk it towards him. It was absurd to be doing this, and even the can itself ridiculed him. Spun by his finger, it danced out of reach. As it pirouetted away from him his mind, urging it to spin back, screeched at it with a quite unnecessary passion. It merely rolled further, tittering at him. He jerked his arm back through the wire. It caught a jagged edge that laid a zip of blood from elbow to wrist.

A dirty tomb. Rank weed. A tinkling can. Blood. A glorious rage surged through him. Rage was the wonder of the world. Rage was the horse of flame he rode as he wheeled towards her. His fist was raised.

Through the aisles of the trees Gilray heard the rattle of a can on stone, and a moment later the sound of voices.

In a panic he freed himself from earth and propelled himself into the topmost leaves so that he would be invisible from below. Deep silence in the forest filled him with foreboding. "Too late!" he moaned. "Too late!"

But Wheatley, his arm raised, had moved too slowly. In her helplessness Cassandra had lurched forward under his arm and, once there, she had kissed him.

"What?" He drew his head back sharply. The frown of his rage remained.

"Oh," she said, but her face remained tilted upwards beneath his.

"Why?" he said.

"You were going to hit me."

"No. Never."

"Not now," she said.

He searched her face. "Things like this don't happen," he told her.

"Ah," she said.

"They don't, Cassandra."

"I know."

He attempted to see embarrassment in her, but there was none. "Damn your innocence," he said.

"Damn yours, too."

Words between them had not made her move. Her lips remained just below his, and her eyes looked to see what he would do next.

Wheatley, as if intending to push her away, but truly because he wanted to touch, put his hands on her hips. Taking it for the signal it was, she leant softly against him. He felt her hip bone and the hollow of her waist, and their lips, with a delicate moistness, mingled.

After a while it was Cassandra who spoke. "I like this place," she said.

"You are not afraid?"

"Not with you."

Anxiety drove Gilray too swiftly. Cassandra, vaguely aware of the rustle of his progress, let her vacant eyes open and saw a heaviness high up among the leaves. Then a breeze pushed through the treetops and the shadow vanished.

"I think there are ghosts here," she said.

"And you are still not afraid?"

She laughed and let her head fall back. "Good night, little ghost," she said. "We'll come back to see you soon."

Wheatley let his hand slide down her spine, but she resisted.

"I think someone is watching," she whispered.

Cowardice shrank him, but she, speechlessly, had her eyes fixed not on him but on something above and beyond. He turned.

There was a thrash of branches that startled them, but they saw nothing. They each blamed their guilt for turning a bird's panic into a witness, and they put the tomb behind them and walked silently back to the car.

12

At daybreak after stormy night
> – W. B. Yeats, *Four Plays for Dancers*

"A sudden storm," said Wheatley, "and she was thrown between two furrows upon the ploughed land."

"She wasn't," Jessica Gifford corrected him smartly. "She was found in a ditch on the edge of a field of sugar beet."

"I was quoting Yeats," he said.

"I don't want to know."

"It wasn't a girl, anyway – it was a frail white bird found dead after a storm."

"Bob," she said, "shut up."

He was content to shrug and say nothing. Linda Blake had been found dead in a ditch, but her murderer had confessed and there was no need now for Cassandra Ashe to say what she knew or tell of her visit to the pyramid with a teacher. All day his sudden starts of anxiety had been washed

91

away on warm waves of relief. It was, as Yeats said but which Jessica would never know, daybreak after stormy night.

Leaning forward, elbows on smooth peanut-hued knees, she said, "Was it you who was responsible for working those girls up this morning?"

"Worked them up? What *are* you saying, Miss Gifford?"

"It's no surprise to me, Bob Wheatley, that you are a teacher. You've never left school, have you? You are infantile – still saying naughty things like any other of the young yobs here."

"Oh, Miss Gifford, you have a lovely cruel tongue."

"A girl is dead, Bob Wheatley."

He kept forgetting, half-forgetting, letting the ugly, oily thought slip in and out of his mind. He could not meet Jessica Gifford's steady stare. "She was a nice kid," he said. "Quite pretty, everyone thought."

Jessica drew in her breath. "Not that her looks have anything to do with it."

But her sex did. Wheatley said nothing, and Jessica took it to mean that he felt shamed, and she spoke more gently. "No, but really, Bob, they did make a ridiculous display when the head said that a girl had been killed. Sobbing and wailing, it's a wonder they didn't pull their hair out."

That was more like the hard-bitten Jessica he knew. The bitch. "Quite natural," he said.

"Nothing to do with me."

"I was a bit hard on you, was I, Bobby?"

"Very decent of you to say so, Jessica."

A fat figure wearing a blue track suit came in from the playing field. She disposed herself over two chairs, feet up, took out a packet of cigarettes, lit up and inhaled. "Gawd, I needed this. Fetch us a cup of coffee, Bob, me old darling."

He got to his feet. "With or without, Marjorie?"

The PE teacher laughed, rasping smoke. "With everything, you stupid berk, don't you know that by now? See me after school." She watched him walk away. "Ain't he lovely, though?"

"Some think so," Jessica replied.

"But it don't seem right to be saying things like that this morning. Not after what happened."

"We are all shocked. The head told us we were." Her irony was lost on Marjorie.

"But he's right, Jessica. I've just had one lot out on the hockey field, and could I get them to do anything? – could I hell. They missed the ball every time, then threw down their sticks and bawled like kids."

"Which is what they are, more or less."

"She was sexually assaulted." A large intake of smoke for emphasis. "That's what they say."

"The police? They love saying that."

"But she must have been, I reckon. You don't go to the woods late at night with a feller and then get killed without there's some how's-your-father mixed up in it."

"Or not."

"I don't see what you're gettin' at, Jessie."

"She may have withheld her favours, and annoyed him."

"Oh, yeah." Marjorie nodded. "Thanks, Bob." She took her cup and sipped. "Lovely. They say there was hardly a drop of blood left in her body. He must have been in a frenzy."

"A frenzied sexual attack." Jessica smoothed her already smooth black skirt. "That's what they'll say in the papers, isn't that so, Bob? – you're the expert." He sometimes got into print in one of the freesheets, reporting cricket matches.

"Our Sex Orgy Correspondent." Marjorie, head over cup, vented smoke into liquid. "Cor."

Wheatley smiled thinly and walked to the door.

"Have I said something?" Marjorie inhaled in a panic. "Oh, bugger, what have I gone and done now? He's offended."

"Don't worry about it, Marje," said Jessica. "His teen hareem will soon put it right."

13

"Please, your honours," said he, "I'm able,
By means of a secret charm, to draw
All creatures living beneath the sun,
That creep, or swim, or fly, or run,
After me so as you never saw!"
— Robert Browning, *The Pied Piper of Hamelin*

A bit of broken glass at the kerbside cut through the wall of Bob Wheatley's cycle tyre and gave him a puncture. He welcomed it; it was a joy, something that could be made good. There was certainty to it. There was no innuendo in a puncture, no cackle of teen hareems, no moping schoolgirls yearning for love, no murder, no suspicion, no guilt, no night sweats, nothing. A puncture was a lovely thing.

He was pushing his limping machine along High Street towards the Market Place when a breathless figure, catching up from behind, began to keep pace with him. Gilray, perspiring in his overcoat, had just come out of Safeway with a carrier bag in one hand and a walking-stick in the other but nevertheless managed to raise his hat with great courtesy. "My dear old mate," he said sympathetically, "I see you have a wee bitty problem."

Wheatley nodded. Where did dear old mate come from, and on what justification? They had met only once, in the library when Gilray had been climbing the shelves. Now they were fellow eccentrics.

"Do you love machinery, Mr Wheatley?"

"Only when it works."

Gilray gave out a shrill Billy Bunter titter that made Wheatley shy away and cross the road, hoping to put him behind. He began to thread his way between the parked cars on the square, but somehow Gilray got ahead and blocked the path. He had shifted his carrier bag and stick to the same hand, and with the other was stroking the shining snout of the nearest motor. "Worth a few quid, I shouldn't half think," he said. "A beautiful old bus. Top hole, indeed."

"It looks new to me." Any car that shone was new to Wheatley.

"New!" Gilray's pudgy hand flew to his brow. "Yes, yes, new – a Jaguar XJ. New, of course. I do apologize."

"No need to be sorry," said Wheatley, "it's not mine. But I agree with you, it does look old. Quaint, a thing of the past – chrome Gothic. You expect it to clang like a steam engine."

"I am enraptured by you, sir!" Gilray swung the arm holding his groceries towards Wheatley, who found himself shaking hands with plastic. "You are the birthplace of pungent insightfulness."

The weirdness of the compliment made Wheatley go so far as to risk the thought that perhaps his mind had something in common with Gilray's. He said, "There's nothing quite as old-fashioned as a modern car."

"Such soothingness in your words! And you must write, of course you write, I know you write." Gilray looked wistfully into Wheatley's face. "Do you write? Am I right?"

Just as Wheatley was beginning to enjoy the wild lift-off of Gilray's mind they had sideslipped into the trough that always awaited him. Writing. The pages that lay on his desk, the stacks that grew on top of his wardrobe, the tortured fantasies that would never coalesce and become books. "I try," he said, and instantly wished he had lied.

"And what do you write?"

"It's just a story," he said. It was also heart's blood.

"Excuse, please?"

The fat face was puzzled, and Wheatley was suddenly irritated beyond endurance. "Why do you talk like that – as if you didn't know the language?"

Alarm made Gilray's face even more childish, but he drew himself up and spoke pompously. "A thousand, thousand apologies, my dear young fellow-me-lad."

"You're at it again. For God's sake talk as if you meant it!" Wheatley heard the teacher in his voice, and Gilray, like a pupil who was still half defiant but did not wish to risk further wrath, gazed up into the sky. "I'm sorry," said Wheatley. "There was no call for that."

Gilray made a gesture with his stick to put the whole matter behind them. "Science fiction, you say."

"I didn't. I just said a story."

"But with science in it. You like machines."

"I like bikes. I understand bikes."

"You have a car?"

"Only because the roads don't move."

Gilray was delighted. "Moving roads! How I long to read what you have written!"

"It wouldn't take you long. There's not much of it." A lie. There was a great deal of writing, but he knew in his heart he had not even started. The stacked pages were no more than barren birth pangs. Whatever was waiting to come out still lay tightly curled and unborn in his mind. "I haven't finished it yet."

"Maybe you are too much distracted by young ladies."

The familiar chill of guilt kept Wheatley's mouth closed. He shrugged, and a change came over Gilray. He had very little chin but what there was of it he thrust forward. "So. You distrust young ladies. They are a danger, huh? They stop you working, get in the way. Maybe you would like to dispose of one?"

"What the hell are you talking about!" In the

narrow space between the cars Wheatley jerked his bicycle forward to threaten the little man.

"Tempestuous sir!" Gilray fended off the machine with his stick and bag. "I intended no offence."

"You talked of…" But Wheatley had lost his patience. "Just get out of my way, would you?"

Gilray had the gall to smile understandingly. "Come with me," he said, as if consoling a child, "and I will repair your puncture."

"I'm not going anywhere with you." Wheatley knew he had been manoeuvred into sounding petulant. "Just step aside."

Gilray turned, but looked back over his shoulder. "Down in the forest something stirred," he said.

Wheatley stiffened. The thrashing in the trees when he had been with Cassandra. Had it really been a bird? His eyes met Gilray's, and Gilray paused just long enough for Wheatley's guilt to turn suspicion into certainty. When Gilray turned his back, Wheatley knew he had to follow.

The Messenger office was at the corner of the Market Place in a side street, and it was there that the plump little man waited until Wheatley caught up. A bill outside said "Missing Girl's Body Found". He swung his carrier bag towards it and tutted his tongue, but said nothing, and an instant later vanished through the archway that separated the newspaper office from the tailor's shop next door.

The clatter and tinkle of old linotype machines came from the side door of the Messenger, filling the tunnel and the lane behind with its secret word music.

"Is calming," said Gilray. "I like it here."

The lane ahead of them ran through warehouses to the riverside, and became so cramped they had to walk in line. The high warehouse walls were towering overhead when Gilray, without turning his head, stopped and indicated that they had arrived.

Wheatley hung back. He was familiar with this alley. It was where he left his bike when he delivered his sports copy, and he knew there was nothing to be seen in it except blank walls.

The fat figure reached into a pocket. "I do not expect I shall have any difficulty," he said. The grin he gave over his shoulder showed his jagged teeth and made Wheatley grip the iron framework of his machine. If the madman attacked he would hurl it and run.

There was a jingle of keys, a door opened and Gilray vanished inside. The riverbank lay far away, a bright painting squeezed between the dark warehouses, and caused Wheatley to hesitate at the doorway. Above it there was a nameboard he had never before noticed. It said "The Shackle Cycle Co." in paint so ancient and flaky that it could barely be read. And in smaller letters, grimed almost to oblivion, he saw: "R.A.M. Shackle, prop." Surely that could not be true, the bright sparks at the press would long ago have made a feature of it. Maybe they had. And maybe Gilray knew nothing about the forest. A sudden lightness of spirit diminished his fears. Life was a joke.

He stepped into a clammy gloom in which he could see nothing and could hear only the gear of his bicycle ticking. Then there was the creak of a door, and a chink of light widened ahead of him to show the outline of Gilray entering another division of the building.

Laughter and a shuffling of quick footsteps drew him forward until he stood on the threshold and looked through. The room was immense. Its walls were of old brick, but whitewashed, in places cobwebbed and marked with dust, but above them, springing from the tie beams that crossed the vast space, was a lattice of iron girders supporting a glass roof. It was a tent of sunlight, and beneath it, spinning on his toes, his arms and carrier bag and walking-stick flying out over his raglan, Gilray was dancing.

He spun so fast that his toes either blurred to invisibility or else left the ground for an impossible spell of time, and then quite suddenly the tee-totum stopped and Gilray was himself.

"I am so happy, dear Bob, to be invited to mend your bicycle."

14

A shaded lamp and a waving blind,
And the beat of a clock from a distant floor:
On this scene enter – winged, horned, and spined –
A longlegs, a moth and a dumbledore;
While 'mid my page there idly stands
A sleepy fly, that rubs its hands…
— Thomas Hardy, *An August Midnight*

"This idiot," Rosa Underleaf pointed at her husband, "has made a frightful hash of the whole business." She narrowed her magnificent eyes at him. "Yet again."

Except that he lowered his lids there was no change in Robin Underleaf's face. He stood, hunched slightly, against the bookshelves in a corner of the shop, himself cloth bound, well thumbed and slightly foxed.

"Speak!" she ordered.

If he quailed he did not reveal it, but he said nothing.

"Shame silences him." She turned towards the two who stood in front of her and unfolded her hands beneath her chin, offering them her smile on her open palms. "It was an error, my darlings. Inexcusable. No matter what *he* may or may not feel, I myself am contrite."

Nat Woodburn said, "You needn't worry." He turned to Pauline Withers alongside him. "I'm sure that neither of us minds, do we?"

Too shy to speak, she moved her head, agreeing.

"That is ridiculous, my sweetlings. My husband, the Grand Incompetent, has wrecked your day by asking you both to come here to help us out at the same time," her head came forward as she spread her arms, "and we don't need you today. We are both here ... *both*, as you can very well see."

"It really doesn't matter," said Nat. "We've got plenty to do," and Pauline murmured that yes, they had.

"Together? How charming!" Benignly, she turned to her husband. "Did you mark that, dearest heart? This pair of chicks have an *affaire* going!"

"No!" Nat protested, and then, aware that he had spoken so sharply it was cruel, added, "Not exactly." That, too, was wrong because he saw from the corner of his eye that Pauline was blushing deeply, but it was too late to correct himself again because Rosa advanced and laid a hand on each of them.

"Well, your day shall not be ruined. We shall

give you lunch." And then her eyes swam with tragedy and she seemed, quite pointlessly, to be on the verge of tears. "How utterly dreadful, wasn't it?"

Pauline, confused, glanced at Nat and heard him murmur something to comfort Mrs Underleaf, using her first name as if they were people of the same age. It was absurd to feel a pang of jealousy, but she stole a glance at Rosa's husband. Robin's face had no expression.

"That poor murdered girl!" Rosa's hand was on her heart. "We don't permit delivery of the awful local rag to our home so we knew nothing about it until we were told in the shop this morning. But how utterly devastating! Did you know her?" Her eyes sought them out, and they answered that they had known Linda Blake. "And what of the young man accused of the murder? Is he also known to you?"

They shook their heads, and she seemed mildly disappointed.

"Ah, well. Lunch." The tragedy was dismissed. She spun round to her husband. "You," she said, "will take Nathaniel along to The Golden Lion, while we two females shall fend for ourselves." She took Pauline by the arm. "These ridiculous men, they do insist on their nauseating *pints* at lunchtime."

The Golden Lion had hidden itself in the tangle of lanes behind the Market Place even more successfully than the bookshop. Somewhere the sun shone, but the inn was in a passage into which no golden finger of sunshine had ever penetrated. It had one small bow window under a jutting upper storey, and its entrance was a dark opening that had sucked the door itself inside the building and out of sight.

Even before Robin Underleaf had lifted the latch the smell of the inn, cottage pie and woodsmoke and dust that had never been needlessly disturbed, had closed in around them.

"No need for you to worry ..." the mumbled words came back to Nat, who almost ran into his employer in the dark passageway "... agewise."

"I'm sorry?" Nat did not understand.

"Don't worry about your age. Landlord knows me and he doesn't ask questions. Poison?"

"Just the place for it." Nat was puzzled but the furtiveness of the word and the place appealed to him.

Robin Underleaf chuckled softly. "Your poison. Name it. Mild ale strongly recommended."

"Mild then, if you are."

"Ever and anon." Robin Underleaf pushed open a door that was quite invisible in the corridor, and Nat followed him into a bar that would have been lit by the single window in the alleyway except for the fact that the curtains were almost closed. It was summer but, under a high mantelpiece, a fire glowed in the grate.

"Two pints. Straight glasses. No handles." Robin Underleaf gave his order to an empty room, but the firelight was suddenly extinguished by a figure rising in front of it, and Nat jumped to hear a voice at his elbow.

"If you're eating, I'll speak to the missus," and the tall figure padded softly past them, lifted a flap and went behind the bar. Meagre lights were switched on and the landlord became visible. He was bald and had a large, drooping moustache. "There's a famine in the land. Nobody eatin', nobody drinkin'." His voice blended with the sound of running liquid as he pulled a pump. "I been sitting by the fire the last half-hour wonderin' where me next customer was comin' from. Times ain't like they was."

"Ichabod," said Underleaf. "The glory has departed."

"As you say, master, ichabod it is." The landlord put two black pints in straight-sided glasses on the bar.

"Steak and kidney pie." Underleaf turned and raised his eyebrows to ask the question of Nat, who nodded. "Two. And enough gravy to dabble in." He pushed one of the pints along the bar to Nat. "Cheers."

"Cheers."

Nat drank under the eye of the bookshop proprietor who watched him foxily until he put his glass back on the counter. Then he raised his own pint. "Welcome to the club," he said.

"Club?" Nat struggled to keep peevishness out of his voice. The scruffy little creep shouldn't have watched him as if drinking a pint was a rite of passage. "I've been in a pub before."

Underleaf, rounding his shoulders so that his collar rode even further up the back of his neck, kept his mouth as solemn as a tortoise. "But not this pub, I imagine, and not this beer." His eyes flicked up. "What do you think?"

"I drink lager."

"Ah," said Underleaf. "Bill Styles won't have it." The back of the landlord's waistcoat had disappeared through a door behind the bar. "No lager by pump nor can – not even to take away."

Nat looked round the little room. No cans, no music, no pool table, no bar games flashing repetitive, dumb signals. "And no customers," he said aloud, but even his voice was muted in the dimness.

Underleaf picked up his drink, and Nat went with him to a small round table in a corner near the fireplace. He had to squeeze behind it to get to the bench by the wall, and its cast iron legs rocked on the uneven tiles. They drank again. The dark beer had the flavour of mushrooms.

"Nourishment," said Underleaf. "She's a delicious girl, your Pauline."

"Not mine," said Nat.

"She would appreciate the chance."

"As one woman to another," declaimed Rosa Underleaf, "I think your Nat is terribly dangerous."

"He's not mine," said Pauline.

"Thank heavens! But the signs are he would like

107

to be. I have watched him when his gaze is upon you and it has positively made me shudder. He has an eye for beauty, that young fellow – and for destroying it." Her voice fell, and she handed over one of the two little white cartons she had just fetched from the hotel across the square. "They prepare a rather special mayonnaise."

"She's a desirable young lady." Robin Underleaf's eyes were so green and sly they advertised his lascivious interest. His underlip was wet. "Quite pretty, I think?"

"Sort of." Nat held aloof.

"All girls are, when you're young. Or should be." He picked up his glass and, just before he put his lips to it, he indicated with his little finger that Nat should do the same. Nat did so, and could feel the cool weight of the beer in his belly. Was Robin Underleaf trying to get him drunk? Did it matter? He decided he didn't care.

"Mild." Nat held his glass up to what little light there was in the room and tried to see through the bottom inch, which was all that remained. "It matches the furniture." He swilled it around in his round glass and said, "It's like a table leg," he said, "brown and well-rounded." Underleaf gave a thin, uncomprehending smile. "Very well-rounded," Nat repeated.

"So is your young lady," said Underleaf.

"If you say so." Nat drained his glass.

The flap in the bar was raised, and Bill Styles

came to the table carrying two large white plates and a handful of cutlery.

"There you are, gents." He put the two hot plates on to the wooden table top and dumped the cutlery between them. He reached down a salt cellar and a pepperpot from a collection on the mantelshelf.

"And Three Corners again," said Underleaf.

"Three Corners it is, master." Styles took their glasses to the bar and began to draw two more pints.

"Three Corners?" said Nat.

"Mirror, mirror on the wall; look, and it will tell you all." Underleaf was puffing his lips in and out, amused.

"Which…?" and then Nat saw it. There was only one mirror in the room, and that was behind the bar. It had the name of a brewery emblazoned on it in gilt letters, and also the brewery's symbol, a geometric figure in yellow. A pyramid, maybe. No, merely a triangle. Three corners. "Ah!" said Nat. "I thought you and old whatnot were in a Magic Circle or something."

"Mayhap we are."

"I've never heard of Three Corners beer."

"That's because you don't know Bill Styles. We in The Golden Lion have our little ways." The landlord returned with two full glasses. "Lovely drop of Threes today, Bill."

"Anything else, just give me a rap." The landlord disappeared.

"He doesn't say a lot," said Nat.

"He thinks," said Underleaf.

The plates were piled high. Greens and mashed potatoes made twin peaks alongside domes of suet crust that steamed like volcanoes and oozed a subterranean gravy. "Also well-rounded," said Robin Underleaf, and Nat looked up into the narrow gleam of an eye that had, in fact, missed nothing.

It was unnerving to eat with Rosa Underleaf. She related in detail the trouble she had had to take to persuade the staff at the Sandringham Hotel to prepare the sandwiches to her liking and now, while Pauline was still eating, she disdained to finish them. Instead, with a smile as wide and white as the meringues she placed on the desk, she said, "And now for two little naughties!"

Pauline was cowardly. Meringues were difficult; she'd get cream on her nose. "I don't think I can manage one," she said, and cringed. "Managing one" was as crude as saying she was full up.

"My precious dove!" Rosa was alarmed. "Are you yearning?" She awaited a reply.

"Am I?" Pauline looked into her lap. "I mean I don't know what you mean."

"Oh, you are so shy. How sweet!" Rosa's eyes melted. "You are just a mite lovelorn, *n'est-ce pas*?"

"It's not that." Pauline knew she should have simply said no. Now she would be misunderstood.

"I see roses blooming in your cheeks."

It was anger with herself that had made Pauline redden, and that was impossible for her to explain. She had to remain silent.

"Brutes!" Rosa flung herself back in her chair. "Men! They have the sensitivity of kine and the foul longings of vampires!"

Robin Underleaf cut crust, lifted pie to his mouth and chewed before he spoke. "I gather you are interested?" He continued to be busy with his plate.

"Am I?"

Underleaf, snuffling over his gravy, half choked and had to reach for his beer.

"I have amused you," said Nat.

"Nowhere near as much as you would amuse my wife." Underleaf made a small clawing movement in the air to keep Nat silent. "She has a woman's perceptions – which are not a man's, *hein*? Where we blunder around in the dark, she has the eye of an owl."

Nat ate. The beer had made him very hungry, and swallowing pie was better than trying to think of something to say.

"You are attracted to the girl," said Underleaf. "Very, says my wife, although she doubts if you are aware of it."

Nat, forking food, was curt. "She's right."

Underleaf shrugged. "Whatever may be the truth of that matter, the obverse is very plain for all to see. The girl has a severe heartache for you.

And I have a proposition to make."

"In their arrogance," Rosa declared, "they think they cannot be led. Ha! We have the one sure lure they cannot resist, poor boobies. Our sex is our witchcraft."

Pauline longed for the white, collapsing sugariness of the meringue and the slippery caress of cream, but she could not lift it to her lips with Rosa as audience.

"A whiff of our femaleness and they are lost – is that not so?"

The arched eyebrows once again demanded an answer, but once again Pauline could only murmur.

"Do but consider that pathetic object, my husband." Rosa waved a hand as if she were wafting thistledown. "At the first sight of your pretty face he panted like a dog. I caught the loathsome animal with his tongue lolling out. Isn't that just too repellent?"

A jolt of embarrassment made Pauline's hand reach for the meringue. She bit it, and sugar dust flew into her nose and made her sneeze. She apologized, her eyes watering, but Rosa hardly noticed. "You do know of his beastly practices, don't you?"

Pauline ate, eyes lowered, fumbling for a napkin.

"Beastly but feeble. He believes he can raise the dead! He has had his heart set on it, poor lamb, ever since he discovered some silly tomb hidden away in the woods, and he is convinced a ghost will make its appearance if the right conditions are fulfilled!" Her voice had been rising until it ended in a yelp of laughter. "Do you know what he needs?"

Pauline now welcomed the white crumbs on her lips. Wiping them away prevented her answering.

"He needs a girl! ... and simply because the old monster in the tomb had a penchant for girls, and my sweet hubby thinks he can be persuaded to show himself only to a young lady. Such stuff and nonsense." She lowered her voice. "But don't be surprised, my dear, if he asks you to accompany him at some time to the ghastly place. Say no!"

She laughed, and Pauline laughed with her.

"Do you believe in ghosts?" Robin Underleaf asked.

Nat drank. "Do you?"

"I should like to discover if they exist."

"You mentioned you had a proposition," said Nat.

"I'd like to perform an experiment." The proprictor's eyes ceased wandering and steadied on Nat's face. "Unfortunately a young lady is needed." He paused, watching for Nat's reaction.

"So?"

"A really *young* young lady, a girl." Underleaf snuffled. "And a person of my age cannot afford to approach young members of the fair sex with proposals of that nature in this day and age."

"Not in any day or age."

Robin Underleaf's eyes slid sideways and down,

and when he spoke he mumbled. "Another drink?"

"If you like." Nat put down his empty glass. He could see right through this creepy little gravy-gobbler. "You want me to stand in for you, is that it?"

Underleaf, even when he stood up, a pint glass in either hand, was not an imposing spectacle. "Well," he said softly, "she is already head over heels in love with you."

"Sweets for the sweet." Rosa separated the two halves of her own meringue, and proffered one to Pauline, who took it. "And of course, the girl must be a virgin." She came as close to a giggle as she ever could. "And I'm quite convinced that you are."

15

On four-horse coach, whose luggage pierced the sky,
... it was thus from school
I homeward came some forty years gone by.
Thus two long days and one long night I rode,
Stage after stage, till the last change of team
Stopp'd, splash'd and panting, at my sire's abode.
How nowaday from school comes home my son?
Through duct and tunnel by a puff of steam,
Shot like a pellet from his own pop-gun.

– R. E. Egerton Warburton, *Poems*, 1877

"This puncture is very deep," said Gilray.

"Deep enough to let all the air out," Wheatley replied.

They both clicked their tongues, *tch-tch*, and shook their heads, but Gilray was genuinely solemn. "Air is as thin as thought," he said, "there's no holding it."

Wheatley, in no mood for whimsy, sighed and Gilray looked up from the tyre he was pressing, but Wheatley turned away to gaze over the wide floor of the vast, empty room. It was furnished with a single object, a workbench, which occupied the corner where they stood. Everything else was white light from the roof and whitewashed walls. "I didn't know this place existed," he said.

"Fur and feather," said Gilray. "It was a warehouse for a merchant's bales of chicken pluckings until I purchased and improved."

Hence the smell of a whitewashed chicken run. "But why a glass roof?" Wheatley asked.

"For the intricacies of cycle maintenance. And for other purposes at other times space is a needful thing." Gilray lifted Wheatley's machine and hung it on two hooks that dangled on long chains from girders high overhead.

"It's big for a workshop," said Wheatley. "More like a railway station."

"Very like, indeed." Gilray was nodding. "Leave here for far away places, or not so far away if you prefer. Standing still may be prime for adventure." Between them the bike swung softly, and Gilray turned to the bench, humming to himself. "Where, oh, where," he chanted softly, "have my new fingers gone?"

"Fingers?"

Gilray, turning, held up a pair of spanners. "Two," he said, "and with fingertips of iron." He fitted the spanners to the front wheel nuts and turned them. "Your railway station is tame, dear

116

Bob, when we can extend our softnesses into metal like this."

"A railway station has much more glamour than a spanner."

"You are so much a poet, sir, that glamour rules you."

"It rules everyone."

"Especially young ladies?"

If it was a pointed question Gilray did not sharpen it with even a glance. "I wouldn't know about that," said Wheatley.

Gilray removed the front wheel, and looked between the rays of its spokes. "Mechanisms are miracles, every single one. They are mind embodied in matter."

"A spanner is a spanner."

"Machinery is the trumpet which sings to battle, my dear poet. It is the measure of all things. Even young ladies."

Wheatley looked sharply at him. "Why do you keep bringing 'young ladies' into this?"

"Because one is dead."

"What's that got to do with me?"

"Her name was Linda Blake."

Wheatley nodded.

"You taught her."

"I teach many girls."

Gilray stooped to the bench and brought out a new wheel from underneath.

"Look here," Wheatley began, and heard in his voice all the intonations of the offended suspect.

He cleared his throat and began again. "Her murderer has been found. All I did was teach her, so why all the questions?"

"One of your pupils is dead and another, I think, is in danger."

"What kind of danger?"

"Great danger. A ghost doth yearn to take her life away."

Gilray spun the new wheel, and the shimmer of its revolving spokes sliced Wheatley's anxiety into fragments. Gilray was off his head. "Ghosts?" He raised his eyebrows at the little man. "Is that a fact?"

Gilray lowered the bike to the floor. "The magic mechanism is ready."

Humouring him even further, Wheatley said, "Magic?"

"With this you can fly."

"In a manner of speaking," said Wheatley, nodding seriously, "I suppose you do."

"When you see an aeroplane high up there," Gilray's spanner pointed to the glass roof, "it is an ordinary teeny-weeny little man riding a bicycle. Wheels whizz, his fingers and his toes do by linkages stretch to tips of wings and end of tail, and this wee man do hump his back and lift across the seas huge loads of persons."

"Quite so," said Wheatley.

"By machinery he extends his little self!"

"A ghost in the machine," said Wheatley and then, wanting to clear the matter up once and for all, he asked, "Which ghost threatens which young lady, Mr Gilray? And why tell me?"

"Your school is a repository of maidens, Mr Wheatley, sir. One of them has been chosen."

"Chosen by whom?"

Wheatley's frown alarmed Gilray. "Not by you, sir teacher. No, not at all. You are a man of honour, I do heartily believe."

"Then why are you speaking to me about it?"

Gilray was hesitant. "There is a person of extreme prettiness known to you..."

"What are you saying, Gilray?"

"Please do not glare so! I quiver before you like a young one. I accuse you of nothing. I accuse wicked ghost alone, who devours maidens."

The words calmed the beat of Wheatley's heart. There could be no risk to Cassandra or himself from someone who spoke seriously of ghosts. To humour the little man he said, "I think the girl, whoever she is, will be safe."

"But, sir, you could help me."

Wheatley, determined that he would not be Gilray's assistant, looked down at his refurbished bicycle. At least the pudgy madman seemed to have done a good job on it. "How much do I owe you?" he asked.

Gilray, aware that he had been snubbed, was crestfallen. "Test drive first," he said, and swept his arm to indicate the open floor.

Wheatley mounted. Gilray's extravagances were a huge absurdity. Ghosts and magic machinery.

Only a failing mind would have connected all of that with the tragedy of a murdered girl. Wheatley changed the subject to more mundane matters. "Why do you call yourself R.A.M. Shackle?" he asked.

"To keep customers away, my dear Bob."

"Then why a name at all?"

"My little joke. I need my little joke."

Wheatley began to ride. "There's nothing ramshackle about this new wheel, Gilray," he called out.

"But my life is deep in ramshackleness, dear sir."

"Whose isn't?" It was too glib a remark, and Wheatley immediately regretted it. The little man, standing alone, seemed suddenly so withdrawn and forlorn that he rode towards him and drew up alongside. "You must tell me how much I owe you, Mr Gilray."

"Sir," said Gilray, "you owe me nothing. I am no true mechanic. I know not what I do. I mend bicycles and I can cook pies of great scrumptiousness, but beyond that I stumble and fall." He paused and then, as if gathering himself for a final fling of defiance, he added, "But once upon a twice, my dear good man, instead of falling I fly!"

He glared at Wheatley with a look that implored understanding but was at the same time so sure of rejection that Wheatley was touched. "I thought I saw you flying when I followed you into this room," he said gently. "When you were spinning round."

"You saw me hover?"

"When you were spinning around, yes." It was true that the little man had given the illusion of leaving the ground.

Gilray's face lit up, yet he was puzzled. "I did not know," he said. "I did not mean to do it. Yet you saw?"

"It seemed so." Wheatley was wary.

Gilray gazed into his eyes for a long time, as if calculating, before he said, "I could show you flying, but do not tempt me. My energy is too precious and time is too pressing for flying games, and yet I need you, Bob, old boy. Great nastiness is in store and ready to scoop up some young and innocent damsel, and I do not know where to search except in school. You know important details, Mr Wheatley."

"What do I know?"

"You know girls, Mr Teacher, sir. You know many young girls. You could be my guide."

"Oh no!" Wheatley held up a hand. "Don't drag me into this. It's nothing to do with me." Now was the time to leave. He turned the handlebars.

"Wait, Mr Wheatley! I mean no indecency. I wish to rescue some young madam."

The inappropriate word forced a smile from Wheatley. "You hope to save her from a ghost, is that right?"

"Correct in every detail, dearest sir. But you do not believe me." His shoulders drooped but not, it seemed, in dejection. He was thinking. Suddenly he looked up. "Proof," he said. "Proof is needed by mortal men. No tricks, no fakery... If I flew, your mind would see only itsy-bitsy trickeries. So shall I show you all, Wheatley? Shall I show you wonders unimaginable? Are you willing to wander with me and know my secrets?"

Wheatley glanced at his watch. "Will it take long?"

Laughter suddenly creased the unwashed cheeks. "Time?" he cried. "Just a tick!" Still laughing, he added, "But pray conclude test ride. One jolly thing at a time, I think."

Humouring him now in earnest, Wheatley began to ride, circling the wide floor.

"It is nice, Mr Wheatley?"

It was exhilarating to sweep at speed around this wall-enclosed, private amphitheatre with no sound other than the silence-enhancing shimmer of whirling spokes.

An age of silent cycling went by.

"Bob?" From far away.

"Yes."

"Did you ever ..."

"What?"

"... play with trains?"

"Loved them." In a slap-happy, dreamy way, as a boy, head on the floor, watching the wheels go by. Imagining. "Never had space for much of a layout, though."

"Is this floor large enough, Master Wheatley?"

"It would be miraculous," Wheatley called

across the room. "Bridges and tunnels, and tracks at different levels."

"And countryside – real scenery?"

"Yes." Wheatley saw forests of stiff trees made of painted sponge, ploughed fields with corduroy ridges, a church glued into a hillside. He knew the church, the painted cardboard, detail finnicked and invented until it was more real than real. "Lights inside," he said. Tiny bulbs, flimsily held by hidden paper clips, throwing genuine shadows in their feeble orange glow.

"A town," said Gilray. "There's a town."

Rooftops. Streets. Alleyways that could only be penetrated from above, unless, shrinking until you were no larger than a fingernail, you moved among the cardboard houses, believing and not believing that the sand glued to the paper streets was in fact crunching under your feet.

"Please to watch where you are going," Gilray called.

"I'll be careful." Wheatley steered, looking at the floor.

"Don't destroy it."

Wheatley saw the straight lines of the planks sliding alongside his speeding tyres, a narrow road, becoming narrower. His vision, blurred by the effort he had to make to keep straight, saw tiny houses beneath him, and he struggled desperately to avoid crushing them. He began to laugh. "I know what you're doing, Gilray," he shouted across the space.

"And what would that be, Sir Cleverclogs?"

"You are trying to hypnotize me by making me giddy."

"Then stop!"

Wheatley heard Gilray's cry, but he was already losing his balance and, ridiculously, struggling not to put his foot into the middle of the non-existent model town.

"Here!" Gilray's call seemed to come from far away but Wheatley, risking a glance in his direction, saw that he was close at hand. He was carrying his walking-stick, and he held it out for Wheatley to grasp to retain his balance. But it was too late. In the act of reaching for the stick Wheatley fell.

Absurdly, the illusion of the town remained with him. He saw the rooftops and he was descending on them as though falling from the sky. All that could save him was the walking-stick. He reached with both hands and clung to it. He felt the smoothness of it in his palm and clutched tighter. But he grasped on nothing. The ebony stick melted through his fingers, and he plunged blindly into an endless shaft of utter darkness.

16

I don't care where the water goes
if it doesn't get into the wine
— G. K. Chesterton, *Wine and Water*

"I have an overwhelming desire for a pint," said Nat.

"But have you the wherewithal?" asked Roote, known randomly as Square or Daisy according to whim, no one being quite sure as to his true character.

"Leave it to me," said Nat.

They left school at lunchtime by crossing the cricket field and getting through the hedge behind the sight screen. "Your father the Rev would never approve," said Daisy.

"I'm the least of his worries," said Nat. "Apart from God, he's got a lot on his mind – my mother, to start with."

"But she's a very jolly lady."

"You think so?" Nat was surprised.

"I heard her and the Rev leading hymns one day. She's quite a disco dolly in the chants department."

"Chants department! You are Woostering again, Daisy, and I'd like to remind you that insults are permissible only within the family. Keep shtum or go thirsty."

"My lips are sealed."

But at the door of The Golden Lion, Daisy had his doubts. "It's a bit iffy," he said.

"I thought you'd be impressed," said Nat, pleased to see Daisy quaking, and then he recited, "'You will find me drinking rum like a sailor in a slum, You will find me drinking beer like a Bavarian.'"

"Don't come the poet, Nat, for God's sake. You'll only collect a bunch of fives. This place is sleazy."

All he got was: "'You will find me drinking gin in the lowest kind of inn, Because I am a rigid vegetarian.'"

"Please don't," groaned Daisy but followed Nat inside.

"What's your chug-a-lug?" Nat asked, but had to repeat it because Daisy was gazing around the dim room as if he already wanted to leave.

"I'll have a lager."

"No you won't. No lager." Nat saw the landlord coming from the room at the back carrying two empty glasses. "Isn't that so, Bill?" he said. "No lager."

The wooden face with the heavy moustache

126

remained wooden. Worse, the grumble of conversation that had come from two men at a table in the corner suddenly let up as they listened. Nat heard the querulous catch in his own voice as he repeated, "You don't serve lager, do you?"

The landlord lowered his eyes and began to swill out the glasses in the sink under the bar. Nat cleared his throat. He dared not risk his voice beyond simple syllables. "Right," he managed.

And only then did Bill Styles, taking his time to put the glasses on the draining board, speak. "No lager," he said.

"Great."

So childish a remark made Nat feel that all his clothes had become too big for him. Now was the time to swell up and walk out, a dissatisfied customer, but he suddenly had no control over his tongue. "Just what I thought," he heard himself saying. "No lager. What did I tell you, Daisy?"

Daisy looked away. The men in the corner sat so still they did not disturb the layer of blue smoke over their heads. And the landlord, with both hands against the bar as though about to push it over, waited.

With the fixed, self-pitying smile of a man walking to his own beheading, Nat made his last request. "A couple of pints of Three Corners," he said.

Silence. One of the men breathed out a grey cloud.

"A couple of pints of *what*?"

The words rumbled in the landlord's chest, and Nat saw the fingers of his own hand resting on the bar curl inwards. All he could do was nod at the mirror behind the landlord's head. "Two, please."

The landlord wore a waistcoat, his shirt had no collar, and his sleeves were rolled to the elbow. He did not move a muscle until humiliation had settled on the two boys in his bar; especially, Nat recognized, on himself. With the last gleam of spirit he could muster, Nat began to turn away, on his way out.

"Right," he said.

"Two pints." Bill Styles raised his fist to the pumps, the men began to murmur, and beer frothed into glasses.

"Jeeze!" said Daisy when they'd found a place to sit. "Why the hell did you want to come here?"

"Best beer in town. Flat and warm, just how it should be."

"I thought he wasn't going to serve us!"

"Old Bill? He knows me. I have my lunch here from time to time." Nat had to struggle to stay on top, and it was gratifying to see how awkwardly Daisy picked up his glass and sipped timidly. "What do you think? Drop o' good?"

Daisy screwed up his nose. "I don't know, really. What is it?"

"They give it a special name here. It's a kind of code." Nat drank so deeply his ears sang. The warmth of relief flowed through him.

Daisy watched him put down his glass half

empty. "You go it a bit," he said.

Daisy was the best confidence booster around. "I'm into something pretty heavy," said Nat.

"What, here?"

"Only indirectly. But it all ties up in a way." Maybe it did, maybe it didn't, but Daisy would never find out. "It's a girl..."

"Don't tell me it's the glorious Ashe! She isn't about to lay her all at your feet, is she?"

"Let me finish."

"Nathaniel the Spaniel – you've always had your tongue hanging out for her."

"Not her." Nat had not wanted Cassandra mentioned.

"No?"

"No." He dismissed her. "She's the plaything of a pedagogue."

"What?" Daisy was surprised. "Does a teacher pet her?"

"The night before last I saw her getting into Bob Wheatley's car."

"That's asking for it," said Daisy. "He's a rascal is that Bob."

"And childish with it." Nat did not care if his bitterness showed. "Just about her level. I always feel I could change places with him and do a better job teaching the yobs."

"True. Very true." Daisy, the pint as much in his mind as his belly, had become entirely serious. "I see what you mean. All that poetry guff. You'd think he was a gooey kid."

129

"Like you, Daisy. But forget all that; I'm talking about the genuine article, a real girl."

Daisy held up his empty glass. "Do you think that old bugger behind the bar would let us have another of these … if you'd pay?"

"In a minute. Do you believe in ghosts, Daisy? What a silly question – you're stupid enough to believe anything. But I've heard that there's a ghost not far from here that is worth serious investigation. So I intend to give it a whirl."

"You're confusing me. I thought we were talking about your new girlfriend." Daisy pushed his glass forward. "I do need a little something to clear my brain."

Nat sighed, but got to his feet and dared the bullock stare of Bill Styles to fetch another drink. "Listen, hazy Daisy. There's a pyramid – no, forget that, you'll only think of Egypt. There's a monument out there at the edge of these flat fens where a wicked old man is entombed. The ghost is alleged to hover around his randy old bones."

"It happens all the time." Daisy drank.

"He enjoyed a virgin, now and again."

"Quite."

"So much so that he'll come out if a virgin offers herself."

"He sounds perfectly normal."

"Which is why, you oaf, I intend to take this girl with me to see if it works."

"Ah!" Daisy exclaimed. "Now I understand your change of heart."

"What change of heart?"

"Why you can't take Cassandra."

"Why not?"

"Disqualified. Not eligible under the virginity rule."

Nat closed his eyes to hide the sudden stab of jealousy that Daisy would have noticed even through his fuzziness. But he had to defend her against the slander. "No," he said, "for all I know, Cassandra Ashe would have been perfect. She's simply not available."

"To you, you mean."

"I simply didn't ask." Nat wished to punch him.

"Well, what about this other girl? Does she know why you're asking her? Does she agree?"

"Does it matter?"

"I should have thought," said Daisy ponderously, "that the ghost bait ought to have a say in the matter."

"She'll have me to protect her."

"That's all right, then." Daisy raised his glass again.

"But I've told you, Daisy, I've grown very fond of her. I may even be in love."

"I'll believe that if you'll fill me up again."

The landlord, seeing Nat get to his feet, pointedly put a towel over the pumps.

17

He said, 'What's time? Leave Now for dogs
  and apes!
'Man has Forever.'
  – Robert Browning, *A Grammarian's Funeral*

The falling ceased. Wheatley found himself standing upright and unhurt. His vision was blurred,
but he put that down to the dizziness caused by
circling the room at speed and then collapsing in
a faint.

"I think I must have blacked out," he said for
Gilray's benefit. His vision was still not correct,
and he squeezed his eyes tight shut and opened
them again. He would have rubbed them with his
hands except that his arms seemed too weary to
obey him. He had not yet escaped from the childish frame of mind that had made him gaze down
on an imaginary town and end up plunging into a
dark funnel. He was amused at falling victim to
some sort of hypnotic trickery.

"You got the better of me that time, Gilray," he said.

There was no reply. His vision was definitely clouded, and he was so unsteady on his feet that he began to topple. He was helplessly keeling over, attempting to break his fall by reaching out but finding that his arms were still too leaden to be of any use, when he found himself steadied and straightened without effort, as though something supported him.

"Am I drugged?" he said, and this time Gilray answered.

"If you have just said something, dear Bob, please to save your breath. I cannot hear you."

"Why not?"

Gilray chuckled. "If you have asked me why I cannot hear you, it is because I am talking to my walking-stick. Turn around and you will see."

Wheatley attempted to move but the effort brought on such a fit of giddiness that he gave up. "I can't."

"It may be difficult, but I shall help."

Suddenly Wheatley found himself being turned around. Instinctively he fought to control his own limbs, but although he flung his arms wide he was unable to see them. He was raised bodily and suspended in mid-air. He looked down but still could not see his arms, nor his legs, nor any part of himself.

"There now," said Gilray, as if talking to a child, "what do you think of that?"

He was face to face with Gilray, who was smiling at him. "Come with me, my little friend, and I will show you where we are."

Helplessly, Wheatley was turned around. The workshop walls had disappeared and now there was furniture, and pictures, and books. Gilray was walking towards a large mirror and Wheatley found himself moving with him. He was making no effort to walk, yet he moved nevertheless. Gilray's reflection came closer. He was carrying his walking-stick and he was smiling at Wheatley from the glass, but Wheatley could see no reflection of himself.

Gilray stopped in front of the mirror and held the walking-stick alongside his head. "You see, sir Bob, the little companion to whom I speak." The stick was of polished ebony with a silver top. Suddenly he thrust it closer at the mirror and as he did so the stick's reflection seemed to lunge directly at Wheatley. He flinched, but the reflection stopped an inch from his nose.

"No need to flinch, Bob, my old sweetheart. Far better just to stay put and look at yourself."

Wheatley was angered. "What the hell do you think you're doing, Gilray!"

"If you are speaking to me, my slim little friend, I cannot hear. Regardez!" He moved the stick, and Wheatley found himself closer to the reflection. And the stick seemed to have eyes – at least, a pair of small black beads just below its silver handle gazed at him uncannily. Gilray twisted it slightly, left and right, and Wheatley's own head was turned. "Look," said Gilray and pointed to two tiny holes in the smooth ebony just behind the eye beads. He put his mouth close and whispered to it, "It hears and sees, but it cannot speak. Whoever heard of a walking-stick with a mouth?... It's too laughable for words!"

"Listen to me, Gilray!" Wheatley shouted. "Stop playing the fool and answer!"

"I feel you tremble, little friend," said Gilray to the stick. "Are you keen to go walkies?" He went to the centre of the floor, which was no longer bare boards but was carpeted with some material that seemed to have softly changing colours like the surface of a pond. He stood the stick upright and released it. "Stay!" he ordered. It kept its balance, and Gilray stood back and addressed it.

"Time is on the rampage, Mr Wheatley, sir. I shall demonstrate." He padded across the carpet to what appeared to be a doorway that had neither door nor curtain but was nevertheless blocked by a glistening shimmer in the air. "You rode a bicycle a moment gone, and now you ride a stick. But please to keep looking."

Having no eyelids, the walking-stick could not even blink, though it would have done so had it been able. The air shimmer in the doorway threw back Gilray's reflection, and he examined himself.

"Winter," he said, "and hot, as it always is. What a climate of awfulness! We still have no control, even in the vingt-deuxième siècle." He paused. "Beg pardon," he said. "I meant to say twenty-second century but we've had to go the whole cochon and Frenchify all numerals. One of the little sacrifices we have to make in Grande-Bretagne."

Wheatley listened, but only half heard what Gilray was saying. There was a certainty in the little man's voice that had not been there before, and he was dressed differently. He wore a white shirt and cotton trousers which, he told the stick, he always chose whenever he ventured into the sun-drenched streets of England in winter. It was cooler than the dhoti or kaftan that most men chose to wear, "and different".

"When I travel I wear my raglan," he said, "but dressed like this does show off my figure." He twisted plumply in front of his doorway mirror, admiring himself, and palming the few remaining strands of reddish hair across his scalp. Satisfied, he straightened and raised his voice. "Stick!"

At the command, the walking-stick trembled slightly, ready to go. Wheatley knew that it could go; he felt the vibration.

Gilray took a pair of wire spectacles from the pocket of his shirt and put them on. "Walk on!" he ordered, and the stick hopped across the floor to be at his side. Wheatley went with it. "Good chap," said Gilray and patted the stick's silver handgrip.

His reflection shivered and vanished as he went through into the cool hallway, tapping the stick on

136

the tiles and talking as he went. "You may think this a large house for a single man living alone, but I can assure you it is no more than average." He hunched his shoulders modestly, and added, "Well, maybe just a little larger than the common run. I *am* the Pastry Cook, after all."

The hall was wide and airy, and he paused halfway along it to put on his jacket – or, rather, to have it put on for him. He released the stick and it remained where it was while he held out an arm towards where the white linen jacket hung against the wall. A gentle draught inflated one of its sleeves and ballooned it towards him for him to insert his arm. Gilray turned, and the jacket was wafted around his shoulders so that he could insert his other arm. As the material deflated, settling into place, a panama hat descended on his head while, at his feet, a buzz of what appeared to be knitting needles tied his shoe laces.

"Thank you," he said to the pneumatic coat hanger as it retired into its alcove, and he stepped towards the water veil that hung across the outer doorway. It was a silent cascade and was thin enough for an occasional breeze to shiver it into droplets and waft inwards bearing a scent of flowers. But it ceased to flow as Gilray approached and allowed him to step through the archway. He raised his hat to it politely as its flow resumed.

"It is my custom to be courteous to machines," he said to the stick. "They are, after all, creatures we created. Like gods, we plucked them out of nothingness, made them in our own image, and set them to serve us. So we must treat them with kindness. Noblesse oblige, dear boy!" He laughed and picked the stick up by its middle. "And sometimes the tables are turned, are they not? We are the extensions of machinery!"

Wheatley heard him, and was tempted to think the unthinkable. He seemed no longer to possess a body and limbs, but he had retained his consciousness. His mind, that had dwelt in the flickering sensations of his brain, perhaps now inhabited the pulsing electrons of another machine – a walking-stick that could walk? No, that was Gilray's fantasy. Once the drug had worn off he would have no part in it.

"I hope you are comfortable within your narrow confines, dear Bob. It was the only way I could bring you with me."

Wheatley realized that he was, in fact, very comfortable – if lack of almost all bodily sensations could be called comfort. Yet an almost undetectable murmur he felt throughout his body was a genuine sensation. It must come from tiny gyroscopes set within the stick's shaft to keep it upright. And then, following Gilray, the stick moved again, but as it hopped along Wheatley was aware that the movement was no more noticeable than the shocks on the soles of his feet as he walked normally.

Gilray stepped from the shade of his porch into the glare of the sun. His garden was of flower-beds and gently sloping lawns, with a scatter of arching trees for coolness. There was very little but garden visible in any direction, but he picked up his stick by the tip and lifted it as high overhead as he could.

"You will see," he said, tilting his head to speak up to it, "something you recognize."

It was warm within the stick, but not unpleasantly so, and although he could not shade his eyes, Wheatley found that he was not dazzled by the sun as he gazed out over the landscape around Gilray's house. It was flat and a heat shimmer lay like water in the distance, but there was nevertheless something he recognized.

There was a clock tower with a spire. It was unmistakable because of its weather vane, a fat gilded galleon with a ring of golden fishes circling it blown by the breeze. It was the Working Men's Institute, and close to it were the warehouses of the riverbank. He searched for the thin crocketed spire of the Martyr's Memorial that stood by the bridge, and found it. The bridge itself was hidden, but he knew that they must still be within the town. In the vingt-deuxième siècle.

The stick was lowered to the ground. "Beautifully preserved?" said Gilray. "You may think so, but we haven't yet left home. Shall we walk?" He released the stick. "You are now in command, Mr Wheatley, sir. I relinquish command of this machinery to you," and he strolled away down the path.

Wheatley stood where he was. He had no limbs

and stood no more than waist high to a normal human, but there was no discomfort and he found that his normal muscular movements were beginning to have an effect. If he turned his head his whole body rotated, and when he walked he went forward in a series of easy hops. He did so.

No fence or hedge marked the edge of Gilray's property; the flower-beds merely spilled on to the sidewalk, sometimes almost joining the vegetation of the roadside verge so that it varied in width and direction, making it impossible to walk in a straight line. Not that Wheatley could see anyone walking except his master, who was now some distance ahead. There was a roadway, but no traffic, and everywhere there was the silence of an empty landscape under the sun. He began to settle into this dream, however it was induced.

Gilray stopped and turned. Wheatley broke into a trot to catch up but tripped over a clump of blossom and clattered to ground. Gilray laughed. "Anybody would know you were in there, teacher. No machine would stumble of its own accord – but falling is human. It betrays your presence, sir."

Wheatley was unharmed. He had felt little of the shock of falling, and righting himself took no more than the usual effort or usual movements. He could not, however, bend to see his own feet, nor even the ferrule where he felt his feet should be.

"Take your time," said Gilray, smiling down at him from under the rim of his panama. "If you wish to see the works of men, look around you.

The climate is only partially ours." He walked on, and Wheatley remained where he was, trying to absorb what was new.

The houses were widely spaced and not always visible behind banks of shrubs of many colours, but occasionally the tilt of a roof showed or a spreading terrace or a half-hidden colonnade that appeared to lead through to sunlit courtyards. And the road itself had a green surface as if to imitate a river or a placid lake resting between half-buried houses drowsing amid the scent of flowers in an endless summer.

Wheatley went to the roadside to look along its length. The fact that there was no traffic was even more puzzling when he saw that it was a dual carriageway with a strip of paving running down the centre. Even this was cultivated to look like an island with long grasses trailing in what should have been the surface of the river. The grass blades even stirred as though they were being tugged by water, and he leant forward to look closer, allowing his weight to be taken by a bush growing in the verge. It was then that he saw that the surface of the road, which had appeared to be solid, was, in fact, moving. So it was a river after all, clogged with the tiny leaflets of waterweed.

A shadow made him start. It flicked across the edge of his vision, and he jerked upright, expecting to see a boat forcing a furrow through the weed. Instead, it was a woman in a sari. She was five paces from the bank, standing on the water, and was being swept past on its current. She stood quite serenely and did not appear to see Wheatley, the walking-stick, but glided onwards to where Gilray raised his hat to her as she went by. She appeared to slow, and for a while their voices drifted back to him, but then she gained speed and receded into the distance.

Wheatley looked down again. The jostling grains were not weed. They were dry and solidly packed. He edged forward, and willed himself into acting as though he was putting out the toe of one shoe. He pressed down, knowing that the tip of the walking-stick would sink among the grains but gambling that they were shallow near the edge. Then the thought crossed his mind that it was perhaps a quicksand and he attempted to jerk back, but he misjudged the movement and slid forward. He did not sink. Instead, the grains supported him and he began to move with them, drifting along by the bank.

Even though Gilray was strolling very slowly he was far ahead and about to pass out of sight around a bend. He paused and looked back, beckoning. Wheatley at first began to urge himself energetically forward but then realized that all he need do was to move to midstream. He anticipated it would be like trying to step on to a moving train and edged away from the bank carefully until he discovered that the grains, adapting to the pressure he put on them, only gradually urged him faster and by the time he reached the middle of the current he was still standing upright without difficulty and speeding past the banks.

"Too fast!"

He heard Gilray's call as he was whisked past and, in his confusion to reach a slower part of the road, he fell. He felt no pain within the wooden tube but, as he lay flat, he began slowly to rotate, caught like a floating branch in a river.

A bridge slid by above him. It was festooned with trailing plants like a hanging garden and he was lulled by everything that had happened into wondering why a bridge was needed over a road on which no vehicles ran. Perhaps it was a crossroads – bridges would be needed to separate the currents that crossed each other. He was still congratulating himself on having worked this out when he was surprised to see the face of Gilray looming above him.

The fat man reached down to help him up. "I hope you aren't hurt," he said.

"No," said Wheatley. "Not at all." And then, even before he realized he was brushing down his own arms, he was startled by the fact that he was able to speak and be heard. And his bicycle lay at his feet.

"Why?" he said. "What?"

Gilray clucked his tongue and shook his head. "You have had a fall," he said. "That is what you will tell yourself."

18

The sun was down, and twilight grey
    Filled half the air; but in the room,
Whose curtain had been drawn all day,
    The twilight was a dusky gloom:
Which seemed at first as still as death,
    And void; but was indeed all rife
With subtle thrills, the pulse and breath
    Of multitudinous lower life.

– James Thomson, *In the Room*

"But the inquest says, my love, that the girl's body was drained of blood." Robin Underleaf had folded the paper small and held it under his nose. "She was quite white."

"Remove your grubby finger from the page, you nauseating article!" Rosa Underleaf bent over him as he crouched at the desk in the back of the shop. They were alone so she was able to wear the glasses she hated. She put them to the end of her nose as she read, then whipped them off. "Fool! The girl was among the trees – that is abundantly clear, did you but take the trouble to read what is set down here!" She stabbed a long and slightly crooked finger at the newsprint. "Among the trees, imbecile! In the forest!"

"Yes, my poppet, but she was an innocent young thing, it seems. Quite the embodiment of his tastes – and the blood was all gone."

"Gone? It was still there, you sniggering buffoon … spilled on the ground!"

"But perhaps, sweetness, it exuded the flavour he yearns."

Rosa, unable to contain herself, swept out of the alcove and did not spin around in a swirl of skirts until she had reached the furthest point among the shelves of books. Then she cried out: "Do you wish to convince me that we are not alone in our service to the Master! Are you telling me that we have rivals to his favours!"

"No, no, my Rosa."

"The girl was found outside the ring! The proper blasphemy had not been observed! It was the merest coincidence that she and the man were anywhere near the pyramid – they can know nothing!"

"Yes, my angel, you are quite correct in detail. There is nothing to indicate that they were aware of what they did. All I wished to convey was that the evidence suggests that the Master stirs – tempted forth by an act of murder."

"Tempted!" She struck her forehead with the

heel of her hand. "You tell me tempted? You insist on tempted? Whoever *tempted* him could have usurped us in his favours!"

"How can that be, my love? The young man was ignorant of what he did, of that I am certain. He is in prison."

"Yet you have raised doubts in me." She pressed her hands to her temples. "Can you convince me that it was not done with some knowledge of what the Master requires? Can you be certain that he is locked within his pyramid until *we, us, ourselves* have worked his release!"

Robin Underleaf held himself very still and only his eyes, as grey as feeding snails sliding under his eyelids, moved. "Hush, dearest heart. Someone may hear."

She was silenced, and the pair of them quickly moved along the lines of shelves, but even the darkest corners of the shop were filled with nothing but shadows. In the furthest corner they came together, and Rosa, suddenly meek, kissed him.

"My little demon," she said, "you frightened me."

"You will have us discovered," he said. "You are too rash."

"You have made me tremble. Pray feel my heart."

He put his hand on her bosom. "It is a prisoned bird that flutters. But be comforted, my dearest Rosa."

"Your aged Rosa." She bowed her head. "Your old, declining, fading Rosa."

"When we have done what we must do in the service of our Master, he will reward us."

"But, Robin, can we be sure?" The lines of her face were drawn taut with anxiety.

"He is generous to his servants. The years shall be reversed and we need never die. Rosa shall bloom again."

"Yet I am afraid."

"Let me quieten that wild heart of thine." He put his head to hers, and the questions and responses that went between them were a whisper that settled like dust and went no further than the bindings of old books that surrounded them.

"Have you not noticed our parson's son?" he murmured.

"What of him, dearest?"

"He is confused, unable to choose."

"To choose?"

"Between two members of your sex," said Robin. "It is the old dilemma."

"Two?" she repeated innocently. "I had not noticed."

"And you a woman. Surely you have seen the signs."

"Well, perhaps I have. But you must not say that I encouraged him – I have no power to direct where the affections of a silly boy may lie."

"Come now," he coaxed. "You have used all your wiles on him."

147

"Maybe a little," she admitted, "but only so he would do our bidding." He chuckled down his nose, and she added, "You do believe me, dearest heart?"

"Until you used yourself on him, my love, he was besotted by the Ashe girl and her gaudy prettiness."

"*Used* myself? Take care what you say." But Rosa was not displeased.

"So that now," insisted her husband, "he sees charms in the quiet one, the mouse. How clever of you, my precious one, to persuade him that she has the beauty of a butterfly."

"A butterfly?"

"Quite so … a harmless, delicate creature."

"Harmless?"

"Harmless. You chose well. She is so harmless that she is pure."

"A butterfly." Rosa seemed unable to escape the word. Suddenly she drew him close, tightening her arms around him. "You know what I do to butterflies." Her eyes were wide as she stared over his shoulder.

"You treasure them."

"I pluck their wings."

"Of course you do, my pet."

19

Even the rainbow has a body
  made of the drizzling rain
and is an architecture of glistening atoms
  built up, built up
yet you can't lay your hand on it,
  nay, nor even your mind.

— D. H. Lawrence, "The Rainbow"

Bob Wheatley, believing that giddiness was the appropriate reaction to what seemed to have overtaken him, crouched to pick up his bicycle.

"I must have crashed," he mumbled, even though he had not the slightest recollection of coming off. But then he remembered the strange hallucination of the toppling walking-stick and the moving roadway. "Oh, yes!" He looked up from where he crouched, angry with Gilray. "I fell."

Gilray, only mildly curious, raised his eyebrows.

"You know I did." Wheatley stood up, confronting him. "You saw me fall. It must have been when I was cycling around in a ring and we were talking childish nonsense about model railways ... am I right?"

Gilray nodded.

"And then..." Wheatley paused. Before he had fallen there had been the miniature town, and then ... nothing but confusion. Struggling to emerge from his turmoil, Wheatley gazed directly into Gilray's small blue eyes which, as expressionless as the sky, gazed back.

It was Gilray who broke the silence. "Do not be fretful, Bob, my friend, there is nothing unusual in being in two places at once." His plump cheeks creased. "Every lover occupies the one he loves, yet remains himself."

"That's got nothing to do with it!"

"Talk of love irritates you?"

"Yes. No. Love is nothing – everyone knows you can believe anything when you're in love. People can persuade themselves of anything at any time, so just let's keep imagination out of it."

"It builds wonders. No space ships without imagination first."

"No Disneyland, either."

"You don't like?"

"Disney is maudlin."

Gilray smiled. "His little fantasy has machinery to satisfy a dream or two."

"Gilray." Wheatley held up a hand to stop the nonsense. "I was riding a bike and suddenly everything turned over and I imagined I had skipped a couple of centuries. Or so you seemed to tell me."

"Did I?"

"Don't deny it – you implanted the idea in my mind, and my imagination did the rest. It's nonsense to burble on about machines and time travel – we both know neither of us left this building." He looked around. "Crazy place as it is."

"In what form did you find yourself in my century, Mr Wheatley, sir?"

"*Your* century?" Wheatley waved a hand to express disbelief in what he was about to say. "In your century, Gilray, I was a bloody walking-stick!"

"It was the best I could do. I wished to take you into my confidence and the machinery was to hand. And it so happened, my dear Bob, that the minute particles agitating your brain, filling it with whatever it was you were imagining, were easily transferable to the itsy-bitsy bio-electronics of my slim little companion."

"Just stop there, Gilray." Wheatley glared at him. "This is rubbish. Just tell me what you did."

Gilray maddened him still further. "Ever since your day," he said, "everyone has known that the smallest particles of whatever stuff we're made of can never be pinned down – ever and anon they appear to occupy two places at the same time, or to be in two times at the same place." He paused to allow Wheatley his exasperated sigh. "Given a little knack with machinery," he said, "we persons can do the same."

"Oh, bloody hell!" Wheatley hung his head.

"Hell is why I'm here," said Gilray, "and why I need your help."

Wheatley raised blank eyes.

"A young lady is in terrible danger." Gilray's pendulous, soft cheeks were unhealthily pale. He was in earnest. "I know much, but not sufficient. I have come through centuries to find her, but much is to be done to save her."

"From a ghost?"

Gilray bit his lip. "I fear so."

Wheatley had had enough. He turned away and began to push his cycle towards the door. It was all over.

"Your jacket is smudged, Bob."

Wheatley glanced down and saw that his clothes had picked up dust from the floor when he had fallen. He stooped to brush it off. Greenish grains clung to the fabric, and he dusted some into his palm and held out his hand to show Gilray. "Part of the illusion," he said. "The moving roadway."

"Indeed, yes." Gilray was nodding, eager to be believed.

"It didn't work." Like everything else, the dust was irritating. It itched in Wheatley's palm, and he glanced down at it.

As if they had organized themselves, the green grains lay in a row along his lifeline. He was about to brush them away when he saw that they were moving, jostling forward until they reached the edge of his hand. When they got there, they turned and began to move back.

20

Once in a saintly passion
  I cried with desperate grief,
O Lord, my heart is black with guile,
  Of sinners I am chief.
Then stooped my guardian angel
  And whispered from behind,
"Vanity, my little man,
  You're nothing of the kind."
– James Thomson, from "A Voice from the Nile", 1884

"Where have you been, Cassandra?" Pauline asked.

"Nowhere."

"Oh, yes you have. You haven't said a word to anyone for days. So where have you *been*?"

A strange turnaround had taken place. Cassandra was moving through a mist of doubt. The girl who, by merely spreading her hair, could entice any boy, had lost all the confidence that belonged with her beauty, and Pauline, no longer overawed in her presence, had to struggle not to be vindictive.

"Tell me who he is." Pauline was both gentle and ferocious. "Tell me, and we can hate him together." Confidence had flowed into her as surely as it had drained from the other girl.

They had reached the school gate, and Cassandra lingered, fingering the black ironwork. "I can't," she said.

But Pauline dominated. "If you trust me, you can." She had anticipated that Cassandra would avoid her eyes, so when the prettier girl looked to the ground, she spoke to hurt. "You are ashamed of him, whoever he is."

Cassandra put up a barrier of dull silence.

"If that's the best you can do," said Pauline, "you are very boring."

"I know."

"And that's the most boring thing you've said yet."

Cassandra looked up and saw the pleasure of cruelty glint in Pauline's smile. "What are you doing to me?" Her lovely eyes were liquid.

"He didn't stand a chance, did he?" Pauline's tone was acid. "All you had to do was blink and he came running. I've seen you do it, so don't bother to look so innocent. I'm not a stupid boy."

"You don't understand."

"Oh, but I do." She paused, assessing Cassandra. She was snivelling, but she had a pretty, girlish way of wiping her nose. Snotty but still lovely.

"Oh, hell," said Pauline.

Cassandra raised damp eyelids.

"You've bloody well made we swear," said Pauline. "So you win. Again. You do know you are just about irresistible, don't you?"

"Don't be like that. Please."

"God, but you're stupid. I'm paying you a compliment, Cassandra. Because I'm jealous."

"I've seen plenty of boys look at you."

"Shut up," said Pauline. "Just shut up."

They crossed the road and sat in the long grass of the riverbank. "So you've got a secret lover," said Pauline. "I don't see why I should care. It wouldn't surprise me if you'd got twenty."

"He doesn't want to see me."

"He must be a fool."

Cassandra sliced a grassblade with her fingernail. "It's a man," she said.

"Oh," said Pauline quietly. She was not shocked, but a new spasm of jealousy went through her. And then pleasure. She lay back and, through a blur of lashes, let herself be lifted up into the hot sky. A man. Someone who had already lived one future. What freedom to be with him! While the mood was on her she asked, "You mean a man – a full-grown man?"

"Yes. I'm terrible."

"You don't know how lucky you are," said Pauline. "All I've got is Nat Woodbine."

They laughed until they had to squeeze their legs tight.

21

See with what simplicity
This Nimph begins her golden daies!
      – Andrew Marvell, *The Picture of little T.C.*
                in a Prospect of Flowers

The small wooden gate jammed in the gravel as it always did, but today Pauline lifted it so that the latch engaged. She had to shut the house behind her.

Her fingertips were green from the slimy algae of the damp wood, but her skirt was too carefully pressed and too clean for her to reach into the pocket for a handkerchief. She began to run her fingers through the privet leaves of the ragged hedge beside the gate, but she stopped when her mother came into the front room.

Pauline attempted to smile, but changed her mind and pretended not to see the presence that moved as silently and dimly as a fish in the cool gloom behind the glass of the bay window. The

157

gate was shut; she did not want her mother's thin smile to touch her. Goodbye, mother; goodbye, Lime Crescent.

She turned the corner into De Fotheringay Road, leaving behind her the wooden palings of the front gardens that were too narrow to grow anything but fences. Crescent my foot; it was three short roads at right angles, as if the builder had not had enough skill to make a curve.

And the same builder, with the same preten- tiousness, had conceived De Fotheringay Road, but now the little bakery on the corner was boarded up, and the shop next door to it, which had been turned into a depot for cigarette machines, was locked and hardly ever seemed to do business. A teacher at school had an interest in that, Titch Tufnell, a fat, sociable little man, and she was always afraid that one day she would find his car parked outside her house and would have to invite him in. Then he would see the worn carpet that old rugs did not properly cover, the broken tile by the fireplace with one of the wrong colour wedged over it, the bathroom... No, not that. She broke into a run as if the cold water tank sagging out from the bathroom wall had again sprung a leak and her father was trying to repair it with a pan washer.

She slowed so as not to perspire, and looked down at her dress. Surely it betrayed her. She was trying too hard to put Lime Crescent behind her. Her dress was too pale, too neat, too prim, when all she was going to do was spend the day helping in the shop with Nat Woodburn.

She glanced ahead. No one on the pavement. She would walk to the end of the road with her eyes shut to prove she was not timid. Even if she tripped and fell into the path of a car and was killed it wouldn't matter. Timidity gone for ever.

"Do you think it wise," said Rosa Underleaf to her husband, "to leave these two young people together?"

"I don't see why not."

She turned to Nat and flicked a pale palm towards her husband. "He snuffles in the corner like a little dog! Pay him no heed – he knows nothing of young passion." She dipped her head so that, to look at him, she had to raise her eyelids and expose her huge eyes to Nat alone. "Can I trust you?" she breathed.

"I don't know what you mean," said Nat.

"Wretched boy!" The eyelids were lowered. "Do we women always have to bear the brunt?" She turned sinuously towards her husband. "I am addressing you, Underleaf, spineless specimen."

"My dear?"

"I ask if you masculine persons must always bend we females to your will?"

"I think so, dearest. It is a law of nature."

"Loathsome, loathsome, loathsome!" Her eyes, beneath their heavy lids, looked sidelong at Nat. "You, too, are a beastly creature," she said. "You

159

pretend not to know the power that a handsome face has over a young girl," she tilted her head upwards so that her slender neck was offered to him, "let alone a grown woman."

"He knows, my dear," said her husband.

"He knows!" she echoed hollowly.

"Since you informed me, my dearest, of his attractiveness to persons of your sex, I have noted the way the young lady looks at him."

"And how, pray, does she do that?"

"Meltingly."

Her voice rose. "Can I believe my ears? *Meltingly!*"

"And she is one of the prettiest girls we have ever employed."

His wife glared at him. "No one sought your opinion, oaf! It is worthless compared to that of a female. How do you know that she *melts*? Only another *female* knows whether or not she deliquesces."

"And does she?"

His impertinence demanded another outburst, but it did not come. Instead, Rosa addressed herself to Nat alone. "Young prince," she said, "be kind to her."

"Of course I shall," said Nat. "Pauline's a nice girl."

"Unsullied. I would not have her harmed."

"She will come to no harm from me."

Rosa put out a hand and took his. "I have your word?"

"I promise."

"Dear boy." She bent her head over his hand. "You shall have your reward," and her lips touched his palm.

Pauline had walked the pavement to the road's end with her eyes shut. It was proof that the day would go well. But she had expected the proprietors to be in the shop to give them instructions, and was surprised to find Nat alone.

"They don't expect us to do *everything*, do they?" she asked.

"It depends what you mean by everything."

Their eyes met, and she blushed. The pavement test was a grain of dust and blew away.

"Don't worry, Pauline," he said languidly, gazing along the rows of shelves. "I've been given instructions on how to behave towards you."

Anger took her by surprise, but he did not see it. "What instructions?"

"Oh, you know … no nonsense in the back room; that sort of thing."

A pile of books hit the floor. "What the hell!" he said. He lost sight of her behind the shelves, and by the time he caught up with her she was at the door to the alleyway. Tears were streaming down her face.

I had to calm her somehow, he said later to Daisy, and all I could think of was to invite her to tea at the Rectory.

22

These nymphs, I wish to make them live for ever.
  So luminous,
Their rosy lightness, that it floats in the air
Lulled by tufted slumbers.
        – Stephane Mallarme, *The Afternoon of a Faun*

The class were dismissed, and as they funnelled out through the porch and down the steps like sand running from an hour-glass Wheatley found breathing easier. She had behaved perfectly, no sighs or glances to embarrass him, and at the end of the lesson she had not lingered but had gathered her books and had filed out among the rest.

He filled his lungs and breathed out slowly, allowing sanity to descend on him like a blessing. Her downcast eyes and pallid complexion had signalled that it was all over. She had released him.

With propriety he squared the papers on his desk; then deliberately let his sleeve catch them on his way out and did not pause to pick them up from the floor. He whistled.

She was waiting in the porch.

"I meant to bring your books," she said.

"That's all right, Cassandra."

"I forgot."

"Don't worry about it. Any time will do." He gestured for her to go ahead of him to the outer door.

"I could bring them round to your flat."

"Don't you dare!"

The sudden exclamation, the raised voice, sounded like loathing. She gasped, throwing her head back with a wildness that made him fear she would cry out. He took a half pace forward, but all possibility of action had been taken from him. If he stood still there would be tears. If he moved, even if only to brush by, it would mean sobbing behind his back. He was caught in the gentlest and cruellest trap. He had no choice but to wait.

Then nothing. Nothing but the mustiness of the neglected cloakroom and a faint filter of the day falling upon them from a dirty plastic skylight. She had one hand in the hair above her brow. Her eyes bulged slightly with the intensity of looking as she, web-woman, decided what was to become of him.

He watched as, lowering her eyes and letting her hand fall limply to her side, she cast her spell.

"Sir," she said softly.

He remained silent.

"Bob," she murmured.

His name forced a word from him. "What?" he said. He should not have spoken. He should never have offered her a single word. It allowed her to take a half step towards him, shifting the heavy air between them.

His brain refused her, but his brain was not in charge. As if to turn her away he lifted his hand to her shoulder. He barely touched, but the thinness of what she wore slid between his fingertips and the slope of her neck and in a mist of breath he stooped towards the mouth which she, wide-eyed once more, raised towards him.

No words for a minute more, no scuffs nor sighs, but a silence that with insect feet knit them together and their lips dissolved and mingled.

The terror of vertigo made him draw away.

"A crazy man I know says a girl is in danger," he said.

"Is it me?"

"Who knows. But if we can bear to walk from here I shall take you to him."

"I shall have to float," she said. "I don't think I can reach the ground."

"Beware. The sole of your foot would kindle flame from concrete, fire from the fens."

A satyr with a nymph. His eyes were dazed with her. Within the narrow space of the cloakroom they were possessed by the silence that their breathing made into a lisping beach and an endless haze. His hoof could print that sand.

"No." He allowed the syllable to destroy the

moment. "You terrify me," he said.

Outside they were teacher and pupil, and they arranged where to meet.

23

The feelings I don't have I don't have.
The feelings I don't have, I won't say I have.
The feelings you say you have, you don't have.
                    – D. H. Lawrence, "To women, as far as
                                    I'm concerned"

The thought of going to tea at the Rectory intimidated Pauline. She met Nat in the churchyard in the centre of town, and for a while they lingered in the small, secluded garden that had been made for blind people among the ancient gravestones. The Rectory was hidden from there, just as the plants were hidden from most of the people who entered the garden.

"The parents are whacky," he said, "but they may take to you."

"Thanks very much." Nervousness made her, in spite of herself, aggressive. "That's a great help."

"I didn't mean it like that. They're crazy if they don't like you."

166

Compliments came from him so rarely that she was tempted to be modest and stay silent. But she kept her eyes on his face and said, "Why are you bothering to do this? I don't want to go where I'm not wanted."

Sometimes his arrogance vanished when he smiled. It did so now, and she felt mean-spirited. But then he said, "Don't let it worry you, kid."

"Don't call me that!" Her anger surprised both of them.

"OK, OK!" He held up both hands, palms outwards.

"And you don't have to look like a bloody saint giving a blessing just because your father's a parson!"

She had hurt him. She gloried in it, glared at him, refused to apologize.

He was silent for a long moment, and she saw him struggle to decide how he should react. When he spoke he was pained, aloof. "What's got into you, Pauline? This isn't the girl I thought I knew."

She looked down, not out of shyness, but to hide her contempt. Not the girl he thought he knew? Did human beings really speak like that? She raised her eyes. "You talk like a parson. Did you know that? You don't want me – you don't even like me; I don't measure up to your ideas at all. So why are you inviting me to see your parents?"

"Pauline!" The tone of his surprise was middle-aged. Confidence had deserted the angular tilt of his face, and suddenly, lacking arrogance, he was not as handsome as he had been.

Then she, of all people, had pity for Nathaniel Woodburn. Her mind soared above this silly, skinny boy, a rectory child, and she felt sorry for him.

"Anyway," she said, "they'll be waiting for us. Hadn't we better go?"

He did not move nor look at her. The scents of the blind garden mingled, and he plucked a leaf of lavender and rolled it between his finger and thumb. "You're wrong," he said.

"You mean they are not waiting for us?"

"Wrong about me."

She watched the finicking way he sniffed at the lavender leaf. "Chuck it away!" she said. "And you *do* talk like a parson!"

Anger made him swing his arm in a futile overreaction as he flung down the leaf. "Wrong! Wrong! Wrong!"

For a moment she quailed, but her anger was too pure to be wasted. "Right! Right! Right! You're conceited! You're a snob! And you think every girl runs after you – well, they don't!"

His face sickened with white anger. She knew he was about to strike her, so, in the height of her superiority, she offered her cheek to him. She longed for the blow. It would mark her superiority. He would never recover from it. But it did not come. Instead, his lip lifted, he lowered his arm and sighed. "Where you are wrong, Pauline, is in the stupid things you say." His calmness, as it was intended to do, increased her anger.

"I hate you! I detest you!"

"Let me tell you," he said, "how stupid you are." She turned her back on him. "Don't go away. Listen." He put on a girl's voice, mimicking her. "You don't want me – you don't even like me."

She spun towards him in a blaze of fury. He did nothing but gaze back at her, and their hatreds, jarred together, fused. Neither moved.

"That's how stupid you are," he said. "You think I don't like you."

He had not raised his voice. She also spoke quietly. "Well," she said, "you must be stupid, too."

"Both of us," he said.

Not eyes, nor faces, nor limbs were of any consequence. They did not touch, nor need to. Keeping a deliberate distance, they walked out of the blind garden side by side.

24

Cupid and my Campaspe play'd
At cards for kisses, Cupid paid.

– John Lyly, Campaspe

They were to meet, as if by accident, in the Market Place. Wheatley saw her before she was aware of him. She stood at the kerbside, a girl alone. As pretty as hell.

He approached her with caution, elaborately indifferent in case anyone seeing them was taking an interest. "People seem to be walking very slowly in this heat," he said.

She did not reply.

"What I mean, Cassandra, is that we had better be talking about school matters if anyone seems likely to overhear."

She did not look at him. Instead, her downcast eyes forced him to examine with her the toe of her shoe as she scuffed the pavement edge. It was the action of an embarrassed schoolgirl. Obviously the cloakroom had frightened her, and a tremble of alarm passed to him and made his voice husky.

"Tell me what's wrong, Cassandra," he began, but instantly he drew back and spoke loudly in order to be heard by others, saying, "I should think the library could help you out with that. That's the place to go." And then the woman who had been passing moved out of earshot. Wheatley smiled, but Cassandra did not respond. "Too many people about," he said. "Is that what you are thinking?"

She shook her head.

"Well, there are." He paused, but she continued to study her shoe. "Perhaps you think we've already gone too far, and I wouldn't blame you. I wouldn't, really. Is that it? Are you afraid?"

She looked up at him from under her lashes. "Are you?"

"Of course I'm not. Why should I be?" But her eyes were hidden again. He reasoned with her. "We have to be careful, Cassandra – you and me. You do see that – you must. There's no avoiding it."

Again blankness, and he drew in his breath, aware that his heart thudded. In her present state she was a danger. Her mood quivered on the brink of outcry. A wrong word would trigger an outburst that would cover them both, but particularly himself, in shame.

"But I do understand, Cassandra. I know how you feel." He spoke quickly because, once again, people were approaching. "Don't blame yourself. You have nothing to be ashamed of. Neither of us

171

is to blame. It just should never have happened. I can see that now."

His pleading was cut short by a window-shopper who lingered nearby. He was feverishly silent until the pavement was once again empty, and then he said, "You can put it out of your mind. Forget all about it."

She mumbled, speaking to the kerb. "Do you want to?"

"Yes!" He thrust his head forward. "It would be best."

It was then that she lifted her head high so that her hair fell clear of her face. "OK." She was loud, indifferent. "Where did you say we were going?"

Her sudden disdain panicked him. Then anger. He had allowed a schoolgirl's passion to stir dreams, and his response had revealed to her his own hidden desires. He had betrayed himself to a child.

With an effort he kept his voice steady. "I'm not sure we should go anywhere after all," he said.

"Why not?" Coldly. "It was your idea."

People went by, and her regard, which had been directed at shopfronts on the other side of the market, came back to him. He said, "You have something on your mind, Cassandra. Tell me what's wrong."

"Who do you want me to see?" she said. "Where are we going?"

Goddess into bitch. He was helpless. Stiffly, clenching his jaw muscles, he nodded towards the corner beyond the parked cars. "Over there," he said. "We have to go through the passage beside the Messenger office. I'll see you in the lane at the back. And for God's sake keep your voice down."

"You want me to go ahead?" She was louder. "So people don't see us together – is that it?"

"Yes." He turned away.

"Very well."

He watched the confident swing of her skirt and the soft bounce of the hair on her shoulders as she walked away. Not just a schoolgirl. She could be shopping ... a wife with a husband at her side, under orders, obedient. Thank God he'd seen it in time.

25

We never pay any-one Dane-geld,
   No matter how trifling the cost;
For the end of that game is oppression and shame,
   And the nation that plays it is lost!
              – Rudyard Kipling, *Dane-Geld*

The magic of the blind garden turned into disaster at the Rectory.

Pauline had often seen the rector in town. He was tall and lean and always, because of the white band around his throat, he walked within a little area of holiness, as if he had put on his clothes in church, and his grey suit was a protective barrier of sanctity. She had never thought of the Rev. Michael Woodburn as anything other than a typically bloodless parson, and was surprised, on shaking his hand and finding it cool and slightly damp, that that was precisely what he was.

Mrs Woodburn, however, was different. She was a soldier in Christ, and a rattle of small arms fire came at Pauline over the tea table.

When the rector said, "Shall we say grace?" his wife immediately turned to Pauline and asked, "You do say grace, don't you, dear?"

It was a foreign practice to Pauline, and as she hesitated between politeness and honesty she stole a sideways glance at Nat. He was glaring across the table at his father. "Why don't you just get on with it, Dad?" he said.

Mr Woodburn looked up at the ceiling, looked down at his plate, closed his eyes, clasped his hands under his chin, and said, "The bounty You have provided, Lord, is spread before us. May Your Presence grace our humble table."

"Ay-men," said his wife.

"Have some salmon." Nat pushed a crinkly glass dish in front of Pauline. The pink fish was cylindrical, straight out of the tin, and for the first time she realized what had always vaguely troubled her about salmon. It was the slimy film of grey scales.

She spooned out the very minimum quantity. Mrs Woodburn watched but did not press her to take more. There was already a lettuce leaf on everyone's plate and a tomato, unsliced. "Lovely," said Pauline.

"Good." Mr Woodburn smiled, and his glasses, picking up what light there was in the room, angled blankness at her. "Wholesome food, fish, don't you think?"

Wholesome food. She knew he was trying to be

175

kind, but what she wanted to tell him was … your son fell in love with me in the blind garden and I don't give a damn about fish. "Yes," she said, "I like fish."

"Wonderful topic of conversation," said Nat. "At any moment my mother will tell us all about the religious significance of fish. Won't you, Mother?"

Pauline noticed, just as she had been chilled by the gloom-encrusted carvings of the mantelpiece of the big room and had wondered how people could live here, that Nat could address his father as Dad, but his mother had to be Mother.

"Now then, Nathaniel, old boy," said Mr Woodburn, "don't tease your mother. I'm sure the young lady doesn't wish to hear, do you?" Again he smiled at her.

"Her name is Pauline," said Nat.

"That is only half her name," said Mrs Woodburn. She was short and plump. Her face was fat but hard, like a solid pillow, and had been scrubbed clean of features such as eyebrows. Nevertheless a twitch in the muscles of the forehead made Pauline realize she was being asked a question.

"Her name is Pauline Withers, Mother. I've already told you that."

She ignored her son. "Where do you live, Miss Withers?" Pauline told her. "Oh, I see you are within our parish."

"What my mother means," said Nat, "is that

176

she's never seen you in church. Black mark, Pauline."

His father broke in. "Can't you see you're embarrassing the poor girl, Nathaniel?"

Pauline managed a tiny smile towards the white neckband. Does he own a tie, she wondered, and panicked at the triviality of her mind.

"See," said Mr Woodburn with kindly intentions, "you have brought colour to her cheeks."

Nat sighed noisily. "Aren't they hopeless, Pauline?" He turned towards his parents. "Father ... Mother ... Pauline Withers does not come to church. Most people don't, and never have." He was about to say more, but his mother interrupted.

Brushing her son aside, she spoke directly to her guest. "As you may, or may not, know, we belong to the evangelical persuasion."

"Fundamentalists," said her son.

Pauline put her fork through a piece of tomato and pressed the tines hard into her plate as if holding them there could prevent a disaster. She need not have troubled. Mrs Woodburn had more than one technique for dealing with her son. Preaching was one.

"We bring the Glad News," said Mrs Woodburn. "The Evangel. We spread the joy of it to young people – to teenagers especially." There was a guitar in the corner of the room, and Pauline belatedly realized why it had disturbed her. Mrs Woodburn had followed her glance. "Yes," she said, "it's mine. Music promotes the Word." She smiled at Pauline with the watchful spite of a gospeller.

"Are you a *young person*, Pauline?" said Nat.

His sarcasm terrified her, and she did not dare reply, but his father broke in. "Really, Nathaniel," he protested, laying down his knife and fork in what was for him a theatrical gesture. "This bickering is not the way to behave in front of our guest."

Mrs Woodburn stiffened her cheeks and was about to speak when Nat said, "Pauline and I are involved in a bit of research which should be right up your street, Father. And yours too, Mother."

Mrs Woodburn ignored him, eating quickly, snapping up small pieces of fish, but his father said, "I shall be most interested to hear about it, Nat."

"It's a spiritual matter," said Nat. "Isn't that so, Pauline?"

"I don't know," she said, afraid of what he was going to reveal. "It may be, I suppose."

"It's to do with a text. It refers to the hereafter."

"Really?" Mr Woodburn leant forward, elbows on the table, hands clasped beneath his chin. He was benign, and Pauline feared for him. He was being used by his son, and it would only bring trouble. She gathered all her daringness and said, "It's only a bit of silliness. It isn't serious, is it, Nat ... Nathaniel?" The correction had her looking down at her plate again.

"But I *am* serious, Father. And it *is* a text."

His father smiled encouragingly. "From which Book?"

"Oh, not your mumbo-jumbo, Father. That doesn't seem to work. I thought it would be intriguing to try a different sort altogether. We are going to do a bit of ghost-hunting."

He was giving too much away. They had promised Robin and Rosa Underleaf to say nothing. Pauline examined her salmon and was carefully lifting a fragment to her mouth when Mrs Woodburn interrupted by speaking sharply to her directly.

"And what have you to do with this?"

"Me?"

"Yes, you."

Pauline found herself gazing directly through the round glasses into the grey eyes beyond. She expected to be terrified, but the dislike that was being beamed directly at her stirred a spark. Her mind, almost as if she was being bodily pushed from behind, lurched into defiance.

"I like ghosts," she said. The malign fury in the grey eyes intensified. Pauline, provoked again, struck once more at the same spot. "I think ghosts exist." She spoke with precision. "We are going to put it to the test."

In the battle of the eyes there was no winner, but Pauline knew she had not lost, and Nat was laughing. "I should have warned you, Mother. You cross her at your peril – and I should know."

Pauline was still gazing into the plump, and now mottled, face when Mrs Woodburn got to her feet and stumped from the room.

26

Outside are the storms and strangers: we —
Oh, close, safe, warm sleep I and she,
— I and she!
  — Robert Browning, Never the Time and the Place

Cassandra, waiting in the alleyway for Wheatley to follow her through the tunnel, hated him. He had become aloof, as though he had the right to cast her aside.

"Where are we going?" she demanded.

He nodded, vaguely indicating something beyond her, and walked past.

"You told me a girl was in danger." She spoke to his back.

"No, I didn't. I said that someone I know thought a girl was in danger and he hinted that it might be you. It's all nonsense, but it may just put his mind at rest if he sees us together." He went to a door set in a grimy wall and pressed the latch. "You don't have to come with me," he said, and without looking back he went through the door into the dimness inside.

"Wait!" She started forward. "You can't leave me out here on my own."

"Please yourself, Cassandra."

"What sort of danger? You haven't told me."

He ignored her, calling, "Gilray! Are you there?" as he stepped into the dark passageway.

Afraid to remain alone in the alley, she followed him inside. The door swung to behind her, and the cool, musty blackness that suddenly shut them in startled her. For the first time in her life she felt danger. It was more than fear. Fear rose and fell. Real danger, when it came, was cold and constant. She could turn and run away, or she could face it and gamble. If she lost there would be no pity.

In the darkness she could hear the clicking of the gears as Wheatley wheeled his machine further away from her. She felt her way forward, and from somewhere ahead enough light filtered in to show him pushing at doors as he passed them in the corridor. One by one they swung open to reveal empty storerooms, smelling of earth and old whitewash, and lit only by the dim light of high gratings.

"Why are you doing that?" she asked.

"Why not?"

He was frightening her. She looked back, prepared to run for the door, but it was lost in the gloom. And then, in front of her, the ticking stopped and she heard a door latch rattle.

"Wait for me!" Panic made her stumble as she

went forward, and she was reaching for him when a door opened into sunlight. The whiteness of the large room they entered made her squint.

"Where are we?" She stood under a glass roof with Wheatley. "I don't know what's happening. I don't understand."

He sensed she was weeping and he turned towards her impatiently, despising the turned down mouth and wrecked face of a girl in tears. But when he saw that her eyes brimmed and her lip quivered, it was he who was wrecked.

"Hell, oh hell," he said, and held her hand.

They went together, without speaking, across the large room. At the bench he released her hand and picked up some of the tools that lay there. "I can't tell you what's happening, Cassandra." He turned away to look across the empty space. "All I know is that I was fooled by the man who owns all this into believing ... something." He broke off and startled her by suddenly shouting, "Gilray! Are you there, Gilray!"

His voice echoed, but there was no answer.

"You should keep away from me, Cassandra."

"I don't want to," she said.

"It's not just because I fall for every pretty face I see, but I think I am going mad." She began to say something, but he would not allow her. "The fat little man who owns this place, he hypnotized me last time I was here and he persuaded me that some girl he didn't know was in some kind of danger, and I believed him!"

"Is that the man you were calling for just now?"

Wheatley nodded. "Gilray," he said. He took a deep breath. "And I might as well tell you that he told me his walking-stick had magical properties and I believed that, too." He frowned as he gazed at her. "So now do you see why we shall never have anything to do with each other ever again?"

She could not hold his eyes. She looked down at the tools on the bench, shifting the oily rags that lay there. He had turned and begun to walk across the floor, with half an idea that he would go to look for Gilray, when her voice made him look back.

"Is this it?" she asked. She had the ebony walking-stick in her hand. "It was lying here, under this stuff."

Wheatley laughed. "Magic," he said, "and so valuable that he forgets it." He reached for it. "Look, there are two little glass beads just there and he said they were eyes." They bent close. "Do you see?"

"I see them."

"And they can see you." He was laughing again. "And it will balance on its tip."

He put it on the floor between them and released it. It instantly fell towards Cassandra and, snatching at it, she lost her own balance. Wheatley attempted to save her and they clutched feverishly at each other, striving to keep upright, but nothing could stop them plunging headlong for the boards.

Cassandra was wincing, anticipating the thud, but it did not come. It was replaced by nothingness.

Instead of the rushing air there was warmth and stillness, and she was poised in mid-fall. She strained backwards, attempting to force herself upright, but nothing happened. She was halfway to the floor, tilted at an angle, gazing directly downwards, and the floor itself had changed. There were no boards. All she could see was greenery.

For Wheatley it was the same, but he did not struggle. It could have been some sort of Virtual Reality game without having to wear a helmet. But it was more than that. He waited to see what new trickery Gilray had in store.

Cassandra, still attempting to stand upright, found that her movements were sluggish and she was forced to remain suspended, unable to even raise her head. All she could see was the greenery. It seemed to consist of tiny leaflets stirred by a breeze, but it was not the tops of trees she looked down on. It was, or seemed to be, the surface of a pond.

Wheatley sensed that she struggled, but his mind was occupied with penetrating the hallucinations that he knew Gilray had again succeeded in forcing on him. This time, however, he was aware of what was happening and a surge of pleasure went through him.

At that moment Cassandra felt her anxiety abruptly fall away, and without effort she found she was standing upright.

"That's it!" Wheatley cried. "It's the walking-stick. It has us both. We are both here – or think we are!" He spun around, taking Cassandra with him.

She was aware that something had grasped her and whirled her in a complete circle. She lost sight of the green pond, but the white walls of the room had also vanished, and the glass roof had become the uninterrupted blue arch of the naked sky.

"Don't you see?" said Wheatley. "Gilray left his stick behind so that I should pick it up and be fooled again!" He turned towards her, but failed to see her. "Where are you?"

There was no answer. He called her name, but there was something about the quality of his voice that made it seem not to carry on the air. He had been here before, but still his eyes bewildered him. He saw trees, the metallic glitter of a bird's wing, and the flowing green roadway.

"What's happened?" said Cassandra, but she seemed to be speaking inside emptiness for no sound came from her lips. Yet there was an answer.

"Gilray's done it again," said Wheatley.

Even though no words reached her, she knew that Wheatley had answered. An idea took shape in her mind. Whoever Gilray was, he had worked a trick on them.

"Where are we?" she asked, and the answer her mind gave her directed her to look around. She saw flower gardens dipping down to a broad and silent roadway that she had mistaken for a pond, and a low-roofed house sunning itself among trees. She understood nothing, and said so, but part of her was excited and enthralled and she passionately wanted to let Wheatley know what seemed to be going on all around her. And he was somewhere near her, she knew. She began to turn around to find him, but her muscles were resisted and she was held motionless.

"I know where we are," he said. He recognized the flowing surface of the street, the Japanese bridges that crossed it, and the houses resting in their butterfly gardens. He looked at each of them. Cassandra was doing the same. She felt she had seen it all before; some old, commonplace trick of the mind, a daydream, had taken over, but the illusion would soon dissolve.

"No." Wheatley, although unable to see her, had detected what she thought. "It's more than that. It exists. You are with me now."

Where? How? She let the questions form without speaking.

"Come with me. I'll show you what's happened to us."

She felt herself moving without wishing to and she resisted, stumbling and almost falling.

Relax, he told her. *Rely on me.*

Are you going to carry me?

Not exactly, but we shall move together.

Cassandra found her limbs being persuaded to follow a crooked path to the low-roofed house in the bank of trees. She looked down, but could not see her feet. She raised an arm, but there was nothing in front of her except the shimmer of the air and a tiny bright bird drinking nectar from a flower.

Nevertheless, without visible feet, she was approaching the entrance to the house. It had what appeared to be a hall, or a verandah taking up the corner of the building and shielded by some kind of rippling glass. It's a water curtain, her mind said. A water curtain? The idea was ridiculous. But then her eyes saw what her mind had described. A veil of water covered the entrance, and she also knew that it was going to part and allow her to pass through.

Then laughter, or the sensation of laughter, flooded her and she smiled as her limbs took her through the curtain.

Now do you see? Wheatley was laughing. *Just come with me.*

The hall was spacious and only the water shimmer along its outer walls prevented it being open to the air. Low benches, cut square, rested on the plain tiles of the floor, and there was nothing that could in itself be called decorative, but the whole space had a harmony that made her happy to be there.

This way. The voice that was not in her ear once again directed her, and the muscles that were not in her legs carried her through a doorway that had no door into a room where the sunlight cut wedges across the floor. But it was laid out with recognizable things, chairs and tables, some of them carefully, even ostentatiously, spaced and some at random, and the walls had pictures, dull ones in heavy frames or bright shapes without frames, and books.

Look, she was told, and once again she was turned until she faced the doorway by which she had entered. Now it was covered by a sheen that could have been water but was something else. It reflected the room. *Look.* She looked, and the room was reflected there; nothing else.

I'm looking, she let it be known.

Take a step sideways.

She did so, and there was a movement in the reflection. But not human. It was something she had not seen before, and it was behind her. She was permitted to spin around. Nothing. Everything in the room was motionless, and even though she was alarmed she laughed.

Look again. She did so. *Now move.* She moved – and the leg of a table seemed to move with her. And again. And then she recognized it. It was the ebony walking-stick, standing upright in the centre of the room, and moving. She sidestepped swiftly, turning and weaving, trying to put herself behind it to get a proper view, but always it moved with her and she could never catch the slightest glimpse of it except in the reflection. She faced it, panting.

Us.

That was the word in her head.

Us, it repeated. *We two.*

No.

Yes. You and me. Not words now, merely the slur of an idea – two in one, two in one, over and over again until the words stopped and the idea remained.

"Bob?" She was sure the word burst from her as she jerked her head around.

I'm with you.

The stick moved although she stood still.

Both here, said the idea, *both of us in one space.*

She believed nothing. It was a dream. She tried to wake up. Opened her eyes. Shut them. Willed herself into herself, but even within herself she was not alone.

27

Now that I, tying thy glass mask tightly,
May gaze thro' these faint smokes curling whitely,
As though pliest thy trade in this devil's smithy –
Which is the poison to poison her, prithee?...
Soon, at the King's, a mere lozenge to give
And Pauline should have just thirty minutes to live!
    – Robert Browning, *The Laboratory*

Rosa and Robin Underleaf sat in the large window overlooking the park. "How sweet the sunlight rests along the topmost branches of the trees," she said. "What an abundantly glorious day!"

"Quite pleasant again," said her spouse.

"Curmudgeon! This is the day of days before the night of nights – and all you say is 'quite pleasant'. It stirs my soul to its very depths!"

"Mine too, dear."

Sitting at a little distance from him, she leant forward, raised her chin so that her long neck curved swanlike from her shoulders. "Methinks the night cannot come too quickly. The Master has need of us, and I am in dire need of rejuvenation."

"Hardly at all, my love."

"Hardly," she repeated. "I note you say hardly. I have tiny wrinkles at the corners of my eyes. See." She lowered her eyelids and tilted her head so that her face caught the light from the window.

"They barely show. You retain your magnificence." He gave a snuffling giggle. "That stupid boy certainly thinks so."

"Stupid?" There was a snort in the swan's bill. "Now you inform me that he is in awe of me only because he is stupid." She heaved a deep, sobbing sigh and closed her eyes on the injury. "Your insults fly and blot out the sun!"

Robin Underleaf's gesture was no more than a small circular movement with the sherry glass. "Not stupid to worship you, my love; only stupid insofar as he believes that you, who bewitch wherever your fancy pleases, could ever reciprocate his passion in the least degree."

She faced him. "That, my dear clown, coming from you, is quite a speech." She smiled, but without offering any expression in her eyes. "Nonetheless, I reject your flattery. Whatever may happen to me – to both of us – rests entirely on what that youth does this night."

"He will do as you have instructed."

"But what of the girl?"

"A pretty young thing, I think. She will do."

"Prettyish," she conceded. "Desirable enough,

I dare say, to attract our dear Doctor."

"I am sure of it, my pomegranate. He will be most grateful, and the rejuvenation you crave shall be granted."

"To us both, my sweet lamb. I shall be your creature and you shall use me as you will. There shall be sport, my wicked one!"

Robin Underleaf raised his glass. "To our benefactor," he said.

"To the Master!"

They drank, but she was nervous and she shifted in her seat. "My heart is aflutter," she said. "I have qualms."

He looked at her keenly, and the menace that always underlay the smoothness of his voice rose to the surface. "Forgive me, my willing one," he said, "but this is not the time for doubt."

"Your eyes transfix me." She pressed a hand to her bosom. "I am afraid."

"You have need to be, my love."

"Terrier teeth, bat nose, weasel eyes! You are a creature of hell!"

He crouched "There is truth in what you say, my pet."

"Gargoyle!"

He grinned, peeling his lips back from his teeth like a chimpanzee, and she shuddered and moved as if to turn her back on him.

"Sit still." The sibilants slid from his tongue like a razor. "Be still."

Rosa Underleaf obeyed, and they sat motionless

together, embalmed in sunlight.

Shadows clung to corners in the shop and made it cosy. Nat watched Pauline as, with an armful of books, she slid them into spaces on the shelves.

"You look as if you enjoy doing that," he said. "Making things tidy. Suits you."

In the dim light her cheek did not redden so much as darken. "I can't help it," she said. "It's just the way I am."

"I'm not knocking it."

"I thought you were."

"Not me. I need a little order in my life, with parents like mine – a horror for a mother and a feeble father."

"I don't like to hear you say things like that."

"Now you are being commonplace. You've seen my parents. You don't think I'd have chosen them for myself, do you?"

She said nothing, and to divert him from the subject she went to fetch more books from the cardboard box that had been delivered that morning. All week she had been looking forward to this day, the first they had spent together in charge of the shop.

She herself had signed for the books when they arrived, enjoying the responsibility, but Nat had seemed to think it was beneath his dignity. The books were old and grimy, but the Underleafs had said that, if Nat and Pauline had time, they would like them put on the shelves. She lifted one from the box and read the cover "M. R. James, " she said. "*Ghost Stories of an Antiquary* – is that ordinary fiction or do we leave it on Mr Underleaf's desk to go in his special case?"

"Who cares? And if you really are determined to change the subject…"

"What subject?"

"Parents. If you really want to change the subject," he repeated, "I like your dress."

"I was talking about books."

"I'm talking about you." He had been lounging against the shelves, but now he moved towards her.

"Ghosts." She held the book like a barrier between them. "Where do ghosts go?"

"Damn ghosts." He advanced until his chest was pressed against the book which she held at arm's length. He made no attempt to get closer, but he scrutinized her. "I'm wondering how you dare do it," he said.

"Do what?"

"Do what you're doing."

"I'm not doing anything."

"Except breathe, and look, and touch my chest with a book. Isn't that enough?"

She began to say something, then changed her mind.

"And now your lips are not quite closed. Don't tell me you don't know that they're slightly parted."

She closed her mouth, and shook her head.

"It's made no difference."

"I don't know what you mean."

"Oh yes, you do."

He put his own hands over hers and pressed the book down so that her arms no longer protected her. His lips touched hers. "That's what I mean."

Rosa Underleaf took a sidelong, timid glance at her husband. "Dearest heart," she said softly. He made no response, and she continued to speak in the tones of a child seeking forgiveness for some small offence. "I know you won't be really angry with me when I tell you what I was about to say when my arrogance annoyed you." Not a muscle twitched in his face, and she went on. "What was troubling me was that it may not be safe, do you think, to leave them alone all day together?"

He ignored her question by asking another. "Honeylamb," he purred, "you are not afraid of me, are you?"

"How could I be, my darling Robin?"

"Not just a little?"

"Perish the thought!"

He looked down into his sherry. "Is there not the slightest grain of terror in you?" She did not immediately answer, and he raised his eyes. "Not just the smallest wink of fear, my sweet?"

"Well, Robin, if you really want to put it like that..." The swan had gone, her movements were awkward, and she had become an ageing woman who was sweating slightly.

He smiled. "So there is, after all, just a corner of respect for me in your palpitating bosom."

She nodded. He drank, and they both subsided into silence in the sunlit room until, with a suddenness that made her start and spill a few drops of drink on her dress, he sat upright. "You trouble me," he said. "The girl is safe! The youth shall not sully her if you have done your work."

"But…"

"But?" he repeated. "Do you now doubt that he desires you sufficiently to obey you?" She shook her head. "Then hold your peace. The girl shall go unmolested to her end. The youth shall offer her intact to our Great Friend."

A customer had been served and had left, and now Nat and Pauline leant against the desk behind the curtain. The book of ghosts had been put to one side.

"Someone is bound to come in," she said, and tried to free herself from his arms.

"Let them," he said. "I don't care."

"But I do."

"I thought you loved me." Her struggles, which had been slight, ceased altogether, and her head drooped so that her face was hidden from him. "You do love me, Pauline, I hope."

He had, until now, not used her name, as if to do so would have put him under obligation. She heard it and knew the significance, and yet… "You used to think a lot of Cassandra," she said, murmuring the words so that he barely heard them.

He also lowered his head so that he spoke close

197

to her ear. "That one," he said, "she is nothing compared to you."

"She's very pretty."

"So are sunsets and butterflies, and anything else you like to look at but which vanishes if you try to touch it."

"Did you?"

He chuckled into her hair, confident of himself. "Jealous," he said.

"I'm not. Why should I be? She's my best friend."

"But you are not hers."

"What do you mean? I don't understand you."

"Don't worry about it." He continued to chuckle.

She pushed herself back. "Nat. Tell me what you mean. Who is her best friend?"

Now she had used his name, and she was leaning back so that he took all her weight on his arm, trusting him.

"Nat. Tell me."

"Do I have to?"

For answer, she pressed herself to him.

"In that case," he said, sliding his hand on her back, "I'll tell you why she no longer likes you best. It's because of a man – she has become a teacher's pet."

28

All I believed is true!
  I am able yet
  All I want to get
By a method as strange as new:
Dare I trust the same to you?
                    – Robert Browning, *Mesmerism*

Cassandra, bewildered but believing she was as safe as if she moved within a dream, allowed herself to drift with Wheatley out of the house and down to the path at the road's edge. Where she did pull back, exerting her will and making the stick teeter on the brink, was when he wanted to step on to what she thought was water and weed.

It's quite safe. The idea came into her mind, but it was she herself who, using the idea as a seed, put words to it, trying to distinguish her own thoughts from his, even imagining she heard the sound of his voiceless voice so that she could answer it.

He must have sensed her becoming calmer, because he inched the stick's tip on to the swirl of green and paused until she became aware that they did not sink.

In midstream, where the current gained speed, they had to lean forward even though the pressure of air on what was now their slender ebony body was slight. They slipped under bridges, keeping always to the centre of the road and following what Wheatley thought must be the line of the river, leading directly into town, although no river was in sight. His eyes were on the roadside path.

Cassandra, dazzled by the sights they sped through, had lost sense of him. "Where are you?" she asked.

He felt the beat of her heart, and let her know he was with her, but then he found it was almost impossible to convey to her that he was looking for someone on the path. It needed precise words, which he did not have. They shared the wash of feelings and sensations, but words did not yet join them.

Chasing Gilray. He sent out the thought but doubted if she received it. *Gilray,* he said, repeating it over and over.

Then he tried to ignore her as he searched. But when a cloud of butterflies staggered around them on gaudy wings it was her sudden delight that exploded around him, overtopping his own desire. It brought back a forgotten sensation from a time when he was small enough for meadow grasses to grow taller than his head and blue butterflies had been flakes of sky falling around him. But her delight was beyond even that, deeper than his own, foreign to him. He saw colours that had never been visible to him.

I don't know what's happening to me, he said. *Don't you?*

The reply was so clear it startled him. And with it he heard, or seemed to hear, her laughter. His pleasure soared, but at its peak it ended. They had wandered to the road's edge and the leaves of a plant that trailed from a bridge brushed their eyes. A moment's sightless giddiness separated them, and when he could see again he forced himself to scan the sidewalk.

He was certain that just before the leaves had blinded them he had seen someone in the distance, but the road had curved and the bend hid what lay ahead. He attempted to concentrate, but from time to time Cassandra disturbed him. She repeatedly tried to turn to see something that was at the corner of her eye, but found herself struggling against a physical force stronger than herself that kept her gaze directed at the verge.

You! She was exasperated.

Me!

He struggled to dominate and the stick reeled, but at that instant they each saw a figure on the path. By the time they had steadied they had swept past and had to stagger into the slower current before they could get to the bank.

"Stick!" It was an order addressed not to them but to the tiny machinery embedded in the ebony and it overcame their will. The stick obeyed its master and they were following the raglan overcoat that, even in the heat of the day, Gilray was wearing.

For Cassandra, even more than for Wheatley, all was strange, but her spurts of alarm were now cushioned and quietened. Wheatley had given up trying to use words himself. Instead, he attempted to listen to her. He heard no voice, but he felt thrills of alarm that were not his own, and a bafflement that did not belong to him, and in a short while he welcomed them both, and gradually, more and more, other sensations flooded him. They were hers.

Together they recognized where they were. The houses were not the same as any she had ever seen, but beyond them the skyline from time to time seemed familiar, and gradually she realized she knew which way the road would turn.

They came to a bridge that was larger than the rest and began to cross a river. Cassandra's shock of recognition brought the stick to a standstill. They were in the centre of town. The spire of the Martyr's Memorial was where it had always been and the roads, although surfaced now in green, divided around the slender columns and spire of the memorial as they had always done and the road headed for the Market Place and the Crescent.

But the bridge itself was different, and so were

the people who were crossing it. It rose in a loftier arch above the water, and the people who strolled there or drifted across on the moving road wore clothes that owed more to dhotis or saris than the type of garment that Gilray wore. Odd though he must have appeared to them, he seemed to be popular and few passed him without a greeting.

A man who had been overtaking them on the flowing road stepped off to walk alongside Gilray on the path. He was lean and wore a kaftan, and his tanned cheeks contrasted to the plump paleness of Gilray, who was breathing heavily as he climbed the slope of the bridge.

"Gesundheit, to ye, herr doktor boulanger, man," said the man. "Coffee, we twain, aujourd'hui?"

"Niet, I regret," Gilray replied. "Travel I must."

"Damshame. How many stages – ungrand nombre?"

"Nofar. Ein horizon only."

There was more but it was a singsong jumble of words they could only in part understand, and their attention was repeatedly seduced by what they saw.

Gilray, after his exertions on the bridge, had taken to the moving roadway and they swept past the memorial and were drifting towards the Market Place. At first glance it seemed as normal, except that it was clear of cars. The pubs and shopfronts, although brighter in what seemed to be more constant sunshine than Wheatley or Cassandra had ever known, were as they had been, and they even saw the entry to the hidden alleys. But as they came into the open they saw that the fourth side was not as it had been.

The shops that had lined this side of the market had gone, and in their place were staircases winding upwards to a series of stepped platforms that culminated in a rooftop grove of trees where people sat at tables eating and drinking. On some of the levels fountains played or runnels of water trickled down into marble fish-ponds, and among the stairs there were openings and arches through which people were passing into cool galleries where shops, if they were shops, shone and glittered with goods neither could guess at.

"Herr boulanger!" A voice from behind made Gilray stop and turn. The moving road had come to an end, the green grains jostling each other as they vanished beneath a kerb, and they stood at the edge of the market where small marvels were taking place.

"Herr boulanger!" A man dressed incongruously in black trousers and waistcoat and white shirt, and hurrying along with short, gliding steps, caught up with Gilray. "Beseech you, dear friend of mine," he panted, "I crave audience."

"Vite, vite!" said Gilray. "Tarry I cannot."

The man wore a long white apron and carried a napkin over his arm which flapped to cool himself. Wheatley, snatching a glimpse of him before he had to turn away to allow Cassandra to see what was happening on the open square, recognized him as a waiter, but of a type long gone. He listened.

"Thy pies, cher maitre," said the waiter, fawning, "are master works of research and craftsmanship."

"Ta muchly." Gilray, unlike himself, seemed impatient.

"Thy tartlets…"

"So?" Gilray brushed compliments aside.

"Gone." The waiter spread his arms. "Thy promised goodies we long time no see."

"On the morrow." Gilray waved a hand, and the man bowed and backed away. "If you're lucky."

The stick tended to linger, bewildered by the strangeness of what was all around, and Gilray picked it up. He stepped again on to a roadway, and they slid away from the market into a narrow street where the road flowed in only one direction between crowded shopfronts.

"See," he said, and pointed ahead with the stick. They were gliding along an unaltered street where the shops were familiar. And one bore a familiar name: Felix Gilray, baker. "C'est moi," he said. "Herr doktor boulanger, producer of historic foodstuffs."

Wheatley twisted so violently to keep the shop window in view that Gilray felt the stick tremble. He seemed pleased at the interest his stick showed. "My pies are socko and tickety-boo, as they say. Tempt the tum with a taste of yesteryear. Additives a big hit, you bet. E-numbers a speciality. My crusts break and sag and stick to the teeth, and

205

their delicate staleness is much in demand." As they glided past the window they just had time to read a hand-lettered notice advertising Heritage Pies and Dry National Trust Sandwiches, aged in plastic.

"We must speed," said Gilray, "the sun will soon be down."

29

I ne'er was struck before that hour
  With love so sudden and so sweet.
Her face it bloomed like a sweet flower
  And stole my heart away complete.
                    – John Clare, "First Love"

Pauline did not want him to see her at home. "No," she said, "don't call for me tonight."

"Why not?"

"I'd rather meet you in town somewhere, that's all."

He took a book from her and searched for its place on the shelf. "No need to panic," he said.

"I'm not." But why hadn't she been able to smile her way through this, been more sophisticated? It was because she did not want him to see the cracked and crooked tiles on the kitchen floor, the dingy scullery, and the lavatory that had no light bulb. "Why should I panic?"

"You tell me."

Why should she be ashamed of where she lived? She was disgusted with herself. "I've nothing to hide," she said.

But he saw the timidity she was attempting to cover. When he spoke he tried to hide that she was breaking his heart. "I was beginning to think you had a guilty secret," he said.

"Like Cassandra?" She punished herself by mentioning the other girl's name. She was less, far less, than Cassandra. "According to you she's the one with something to hide."

"Such as a teacher in the bedroom?"

"She doesn't go that far – she'd have told me."

"Either way," he said, "who cares?"

"You do, that's obvious. But I still don't believe it, no matter what you say. Mr Wheatley isn't that stupid."

"Randy Bob? Haven't you seen him fornicating around Jessica Gifford?"

"Well, that's different. She's a teacher."

That made him laugh again.

"You're too clever," she said. "And you do know what I mean. He's too old for Cassandra."

"Who's Cassandra, anyway?" He sorted books without looking at her.

"She's a very good-looking girl, that's what she is," said Pauline.

Still concentrating on what he was doing, he said, "Is that an invitation?"

"Invitation? What do you mean?"

"An invitation to me to tell you how much

prettier I think you are."

"You are laughing at me."

He shook his head.

"And I don't want you to say it," she said. "I don't want you to say anything."

He obeyed her and, without their eyes meeting, they sorted books and found places for them. Not looking, not touching, not speaking, they moved in the airless space between the shelves until, knowing what would happen, she stood still and he went to her and kissed her.

After a while, he said, "Arrogant. You may not know it, but that's what you are."

"The sun!" sighed Rosa Underleaf. "Will it never go down?"

"And leave the world to darkness and to me."

The unexpected words made her look towards her husband. "To us," she corrected him. "The darkness is for us."

He allowed himself a smile, and she recognized that his terrifying anger of earlier in the day had eased.

"Your smirk is incorrigibly smug, my evil one," she said softly. "Why so?"

"I was contemplating our night at the theatre."

She instantly became apprehensive. "You have the tickets?" she asked.

He took his wallet from his inner pocket and patted it.

"Because," she said, "we must be seen at the

theatre the whole evening, both of us together, in view of everyone for every single moment."

"We have rehearsed this many, many times, my love, and yet your heart still patters."

"Because I am female and I yield to whims and fancies."

"You, my gentle dove, are iron, as are all of your sex."

"Brute! We are as clay in the hands of men."

"Nonetheless, our young sacrifice in the shop will resist all the enticements of that thin-visaged youth we have set to lure her to the place. She will be pure for the midnight mummery."

"Mummery?"

"That is what the young Woodburn believes. He scorns the ceremony we ask him to perform, thinks it worthless – yet he will do it even though he disbelieves." He smiled. "To the world, we are fakes, are we not?"

"Fakes." She smiled. "Mere harmless lunatics."

"And have you done your work well, my Rosa?"

"I have."

"Then everything has been prepared," he said, and held his empty sherry glass to the light so that its facets sparkled. "What a pretty thing," he said, and snapped its stem.

30

When I turn away, on its fine stalk
Twilight has fined to naught, the parsley flower
Figures, suspended still and ghostly white,
The past hovering as it revisits the light.
— Edward Thomas, *It Rains*

"My children," said Gilray to the walking-stick, "you cannot talk but I know you are there."

For answer, Cassandra and Wheatley, moving as if slowly dancing together, made the stick gyrate gently. He laughed and said, "Please to be on best behaviour if persons approach."

They had left the centre of the town behind and the houses were becoming more and more widely spaced until, quite suddenly, they were in open country, riding on a bank between flat fields.

There were few travellers and those who passed them, going in the opposite direction, flicked by at speed, the fastest of them sheltered from the wind by transparent bubbles anchored to the moving road. Gilray, scorning protection, leaned into the press of air and held on to the brim of his hat. He had become preoccupied, and for a long time remained silent while Cassandra and Wheatley gazed at unfamiliar crops, and fields that were being worked by slow-moving machines that picked their way on spindly legs between the rows of plants.

At length, Gilray sighed. "Look your fill, my sweetlings," he said. "You are seeing the new world. But you cannot stay here, my dears. One last glimpse only."

Why? The vehemence of Wheatley's question made the stick tremble, and Gilray detected it. "Because," he said, "I am all but done. My little bit of tricksiness wears out."

Again he fell silent, and they watched the horizon thicken with trees until the road slid, whispering, into a forest. It was then that Gilray worked his way towards the slow moving edge and stepped off. He moved quickly into the bracken and tall fireweed, where he paused and gazed cautiously around.

"Long ages do pile up in this secret place." His voice was hushed as if he feared to be overheard. "Centuries on centuries lie here heaped to treetop height and throw deep shadows all around, and we do follow a trail, my children, up and down the horrible long years ..." his shoulders stiffened and he shuddered "...horrible, terrible long years, piled up like dirty plates and dishes."

212

Cassandra sensed that Gilray's picture of the years amused Wheatley, but they had to move on. The setting sun stabbed at the high branches but could not reach the deepening gloom of the forest floor where they walked, and the little man became fearful as he penetrated deeper into the wood.

"A thousand thousand summer nights surround us here," Gilray whispered. "All that has passed is still here – it hovers around us now, could we but see."

He snatched up the stick, suddenly urgent. "Have you not felt that somewhere, just within your grasp, at the very nail-edge of your finger, that the secret of everything awaits you?" He had brought the stick close to his face, but now he held it at arm's length. "I did claw to the very edge of time one night and I found such horribleness as makes a wreckage of my days!"

The anguish of the memory made him raise his voice, and the sound he was making alarmed him. "Quietness is a necessity," he whispered. "I pull hushness around me."

It was the fireweed, its purple flowers tinged grey by the dusk but still glimmering as if they held the last of the daylight, that made Cassandra certain where they were. The trees made an unholy avenue along which, as if falling, they drifted further and further into the long gloom, and the glade, when it came, did not surprise her. They paused alongside Gilray at its boundary and gazed at the dark pyramid of the tomb.

"All's peace." Gilray rested his back against a mossy oak. "My walking-stick has brought us here," he said, "my slender servant." He beckoned, and when the stick hopped closer he spoke to it. "You were made to obey me, but such exquisiteness of machinery has gone into you that your particles are in touch with happenings that are beyond our comprehension. We did not know what we made when we manufactured you, my black and slender little friend."

He picked the stick up and walked just beyond the shelter of the oak. "I cannot fly," he said, and Cassandra and Wheatley knew he was addressing them, "but please to observe me." Still holding the stick, he took a step into the air and brought both feet together so that he stood there, in air, a hand span above the grass.

He was panting. "It is burdensome to fly," he said. "I did not choose to become unearthbound man. And in truth I do not fly – it is not flight you see. I go on stepping stones through time. I sense the seconds and place myself where I would wish to be."

He sank to earth. "I am nothing," he said. "It is my little friend who carries me. His machinery is so tiny it trickles through time, through all its cracks and crevices, back and forth, and he takes me with him."

Gilray shuddered. "Schoolmaster and lady," he said, "it was the frightfulness I saw in this place that began the journey that drove me back through

214

time to find you." He looked towards the glowering pyramid. "Before I travelled back into your time I was strolling through this glade one summer night when I did see such things as I was never meant to see." He drew his coat tighter. "Some persons gathered here were grouped together in a ceremonial that did become vile – such vileness that I cried aloud and rushed among them at that black pyramid's foot. And then did horror overcome me!"

He broke off as if unable to describe what happened next, but after a moment he mastered himself. "I saw a shape come from the tomb, man-size but terrible. I struck it, but its awful hand did snatch my stick and hurl me to the ground. It raised aloft my stick to strike me. My arms were pained and useless and my wits did fly." He drew in his breath. "In terror my wits were thrown far and wide, but in that moment, as my stick sped downwards all the particles of my brain drew to it with a dreadful concentration, forbidding it to strike. I pierced it. I rode it. I was sucked inside – as you are now – by mastery of machinery."

He paused again and gazed into their window, the walking-stick's little black eyes. "Exquisiteness of machinery picked up my particles and in that moment I did learn the knack of in and out, and up and down, and forward and back ... I did dodge through time. I fled the horror down the years before my will gave out, and then..."

He spread his arms as though he himself was

215

amazed at what he was saying, but after a moment he gathered his raglan around himself once more. "And then ... I was cast ashore in this place in your own sweet time, my dears. No one knew, and never did I tell till now. I feared what I knew. I feared the frightfulness let loose by those who gathered round the pyramid."

He breathed the air, snuffling. "There are trails and tracks in time, thin rootlets that reach through weeny cracks and skinny fissures, for ever the same cracks, for ever and ever the same trail. I travel on one track only. From then to now and back again, with nothingness in between. My trail begins and ends in this awful place." He moaned. "I cannot escape, and I travel darkly. All I know is that down these long centuries has that foul beast been nurtured and let loose by sacrifice. The trail is marked by the blood of young ladies!"

He stopped speaking and held his arms around his chest, hugging himself as though he wished to hide something from them. At length he broke his silence.

"Pretty maid," he said, "far back from now, in your own time, you were chosen as the sacrifice. I saw you in this spot and heard you talk of ghosts. I knew it had begun."

No! Cassandra rejected it. It was too hideous to think about. "No!" Her cry was so loud she was sure she must be heard. But the ebony rod was voiceless, and now he was telling them more.

"You are within my trail through time," he said,

"and we who are within the trail can never escape the trail. You would join it no matter what I did. The servants of the beast would have lured you to this spot, even by using nice Mr Wheatley and all his lovey-doveyness."

Wheatley had been brought to the brink of a sickening gulf. He saw what he had done. He should have refused to take her to the pyramid. He was to blame.

"Listen, lady." Gilray's voice was soft. "You and I will alter nature. The beast shall be denied his sacrifice. In your own time you were at this spot by the tomb on this night, as you are now. All times between then and now are stacked here where they happened, all together, all overlapping, as we should see if we were allowed to see. But we shall shatter the foundation of these awful deeds. The sacrifice in your own time will be taken away from the clutch of the beast in the pyramid because I have brought you out of your own days into this future time. His victim is taken from him – and he will fail. Nature will tremble on this spot, all times collapsing together, and terrible events that should take place will not take place. You shall be safe."

Suddenly Gilray's spirits lifted and he smiled. "I repair bicycles, I am a baker of broken tarts. So fear not – your friend the Pastryman has wrestled with destiny! He flitteth to and fro along this path, knowing but little, yet he has found one wild romantic couple so full of dreams that they leap inside a walking-stick to topple the universe!"

Wheatley, unable to question him, thought of one thing only. If Gilray was correct, a girl should truly have died two centuries ago. And that girl was Cassandra.

The little man stood up. "Layers and layers of hideous deeds are stacked up here, but we have played a trick with time. No sacrifice will take place in your own time. It cannot. I have taken you from it, and all that follows in this dreadful place has been changed. The sequence is broken. Nothing will happen this night. The horribleness has shrivelled and gone!" He lifted the stick and rested it in a cleft of the oak. "All is changed, and you may sleep this darkness away while I keep watch."

31

Now folds the lily all her sweetness up,
And slips into the bosom of the lake:
So fold thyself, my dearest, thou, and slip
Into my bosom and be lost in me.

— Tennyson, *The Princess*

Gilray sniffed the night. "Scent of slumber fills the air," he said. "Ancient old forest is full of sleepfulness." He chuckled, resting his head against the oak close to where his stick lay in the cleft. "Once upon a time a small fat pastrycook did miracles, but all is almost done and he will be free of his great task before the sun comes up."

He moved out into the open, nearer the pyramid. "Once upon a time, upon a time, upon a time..." he chanted. "All times stack up and overlap. Wherever one creeps in the other is. In this same spot two hundred years ago the old ghost at this moment awaits what will never come for him – never, ever, ever. Two hundred years ago, as I stand here now, so he does stand and wait in vain for young lady ... and will wait for all time. There will be no ceremony this night. His spell is dead and gone!"

Wheatley and Cassandra saw Gilray lift from the ground and heard his voice trail away as he vanished into the gloom behind the pyramid.

At the forest edge Nat nudged the car off the road into the mouth of the track through the trees. It was dark, and for a moment Pauline wanted to tell him to turn around and drive away, but then he got out and let the driver's door slam with a noise that made her start. She got out and he came closer as if to kiss her, but she gently held him away.

"I'm too frightened," she said.

"Of me?"

She shook her head, stirring the scents of pine and fern. "This place," she said, "this place..." and she did not know how to go on.

"It has the odour of church mould and damp hassocks," he said. "It's sexy."

"You are very predictable," she said. "I knew you would say that."

He laughed, but almost without sound. "I think I love you, Pauline."

"You may, if you wish." She hardly knew what she was saying, but the tall and frightening trees were drawing from her a sensation so immodest she feared it was detectable, floating around her as tangible as a gauze. It was as though the forest, seeing her for what she was, knowing her secrets, leered at her and tempted her. She panicked and walked quickly from him into the shadow of the track.

Wheatley, at rest within the oak, looked out into the glade.

"Dark," he said.

"Dark," Cassandra's echo overlapped him, and they were certain they heard each other.

Conscious of the pulse of her heart, he drew in his breath and repeated the word, drawing out the long vowel and hearing her catch and hold the sound with him. Pleasure ran through them both.

"If we can talk," he said, "say something to me." He held himself still, listening.

Cassandra felt the urgency of his mind and guessed he was speaking, but no words came to her. Whatever he was saying was too complex. He needed words, and what they shared was less than words. But that was untrue. It was more than words. And less. Two opposites at once. She closed her mental eyes and sighed.

Nothing. Wheatley detected nothing. She had not heard him. Close though they were, forced into one narrow space, they were far apart. He kept words out of his mind and gazed out into the solemn, silent space of the forest clearing.

Pauline looked up. The trees made their own sky, peopling it with so few stars that the bright needles

221

piercing the canopy were widely spaced.

She heard Nat stumble behind her. "Damn that ghost," he said, "it tripped me."

Unable to prevent herself, Pauline clicked her tongue, mocking him.

"I heard that," he said.

She did not answer.

"You are treating me like a child."

"So I am."

He caught up with her. "And who do you think you are? Queen of the Night?"

She liked that. It suited the place. It suited her. The moths that soundlessly fanned the air were sending their scents drifting through the night to attract a mate from miles away, and now, with the smallest of movements, she was able to draw him to her. "Yes, I am," she said. "I am Queen of the Night."

Wheatley's exasperation had declined into dull acceptance. Cassandra was aware of his mood and attempted to coax him into hers. "Dark," she repeated, "it's dark." The word so nearly contained what she was feeling that she said it again, drawing it out as though it was music. "Dark," she whispered. "Dark."

Wheatley concentrated on the pyramid. Dark. Yes, he had heard her, but of what use was that? An exchange of syllables was not talk. He closed his mind to her.

She felt it happen. The message he sent out was

222

simple enough, and she, knowing what she did, also withdrew herself. Like a stream that had washed against a rock, trailing its moss, she ceased to flow.

Wheatley felt her leave him. It was as if his muscles, which had been relaxed and indolent, had been stripped of their softness and become harsh.

Pauline found the pyramid and stood still among the tall grasses at the edge of the clearing. Nat went to within a pace of her. "A girl in a glade," he said. "I've always wanted to meet one." She was silent, and he moved closer and looked into her face. "Are you human?"

She still made no reply, and he dared to rest one hand on her hip.

"A nymph? A nymph of the woods?"

She shook her head, and he held her closer. "A girl?" he asked.

She made no reply.

"Not a nymph, but beautiful enough. Not a girl, but soft enough. So who am I touching?"

It was then that she moved. He felt her turn in the crook of his arm and press herself against him. The movement was so shameless that he flinched, and his timidity made her bold. She reached up, drew down his head and opened her lips for him.

Wheatley's mind clung to shadows. Cassandra detected it and, as silent as moonlight, she settled beside him.

His mind was in darkness. She curved herself as if to cup him. Light and dark together. Dark light. His brain, made daring by her, glimpsed it. They rested for a moment and then, like two pools swollen by rain, their minds expanded until they touched and the twin pond rims, fractured by contact, sprang into a single circumference.

Joined by touch, only the thinness of summer clothes was the barrier between Nat and Pauline. Her breasts felt the palm of his hand, and her tongue dared to taste his lips. Clinging to his neck, she let her head droop against his chest.

The cloakroom. Cassandra's mind returned to it, and she drew him with her. She caressed him, moving as she had longed to do then, and very gradually she sensed that he was aware of what she was doing.

He moved his hand as if to touch her hair, and then her cheek.

"Are you there?" he asked, and her answer came in the softness of the sensation of her lips in his imaginary palm.

"And there?" He slid his hand to her shoulder, and she tilted her head to trap it against her neck. He sensed what she did, and his mind was suddenly aware that, without the contact of bodies, the world would never know or condemn what they did.

She lay with him, a girl in the golden wheat, and

his hand was following the long curve of her spine when his mind, intent on her, fell suddenly free. He was in an instant in a void, out of his depth, engulfed in sensations he had never guessed at. He started back, away from her.

He had left her, and Cassandra was bewildered. She sought for him, and when they touched she recognized his alarm. He was afraid of her. She had allowed him too much of herself, and he was lost in her. He was afraid that he may discover too much.

She waited. She did not share his terror of unknown country. She moved only enough to reassure him that she was no more than the girl he knew, and that she loved like a girl. His panic subsided.

Only then, holding to him in the cleft of the oak, did she unfold and begin to instruct him in herself. She drew him deeper, clasping and unclasping, sliding and entwining with him, startling him by having no shame and moving with him into places that had never had a name.

A sharp stab of pleasure began to drain them both. He threw back his head, and the movement tossed the stars in a sparkling band across the sky high above the shadow spike of the tomb.

Somewhere the branch of a tree broke with a crack that echoed through the darkness. Nat and Pauline clung tight, listening.

No further sound came through the trees, no

soft pad of foot or hiss of breath. Pauline pushed herself gently from him.

"Ghosts," she said.

Gilray had drifted among the trees and back to the glade where the stick rested safely in the oak. He was humming to himself, content with his night's work, and he did not see the figures that entered the forest. They began to make their way through the trees, murmuring to themselves as they prepared for their ceremony at the pyramid.

32

And, rotten from the gunwale to the keel,
*   Rat-riddled, bilge bestank,*
Slime-slobbered, horrible, I saw her reel,
*   And drag her oozy flank,*
And sprawl among the deft young waves, that
*   laughed,*
And leapt, and turned in many a sportive wheel,
As she thumped onward with her lumbering
*   draught.*

                    – T. E. Brown, *The Schooner*

The theatre stood at an awkward angle to a small courtyard in a back street. The town may have hidden it away, but its tiny foyer was crowded and bright.

Rosa Underleaf was gratified to see so many faces she knew, and so many who recognized her. "Robin, darling," she said, "the entire haut monde is here, the cream of our small society." He blinked and frowned. "Smile," she urged him

227

and, bending close to his ear, reminded him that they were there in order to be seen.

"Yes, yes." He was impatient, well aware that the Underleafs had to be seen to be having an evening out at the theatre and were quite ignorant of whatever the young couple they employed may be doing tonight. No trail must lead back to them.

"And I beg you not to forget we are here to enjoy ourselves." His wife stood back and, in order to be overheard, raised her voice. "An exciting project – a new play, and on a contemporary theme."

Robin Underleaf wrinkled his brow. Until that moment he had ignored the play itself, but now he asked, "And what would that be, my love – what theme?"

She was whimsical. "Something dear to your heart, you villain." She smiled at a couple who were within earshot. "We are in for an evening of Grand Guignol. The play is about an awful murder – *Buck Ruxton's Saturday Night* – he murdered his wife, if you remember, and then the maid."

"Ah," Robin returned her smile, "how pleasant." The play, no matter how loosely, would echo what happened at the pyramid. A knot would be tied. "I look forward to it, my love."

Gilray came back to the oak. "Nothing stirs," he said. "The night does yawn with dullness." He looked out at the glade. "No person comes to see old ghostie now. We did save a young maiden two hundred years gone by, and all beastliness inside dark pyramid did shrivel and vanish for ever. All is quietness." He gently moved the stick where it lay in the crevice. "Do you hear me?"

He put his head close to the stick, expecting some movement to show they were aware of him, but it lay quite still. He chuckled. "Lovers love to sleep," he murmured. "Young ladies then and now are safe tonight."

He sat on the mossy forest floor with his back to the tree trunk and wrapped his raglan around him. He rested his head on his knees and closed his eyes.

Robin Underleaf, sitting in the darkness of the theatre, did not care if the curtain never rose. His attention was absorbed in the green glow of the EXIT sign above the door. He noted that, except for one, each capital letter was composed entirely of right-angles, and the odd one out, the *X*, opened its arms to the ragged right-hand edge of the *E* as if to collect the unsupported ends of the horizontals and draw them to the point of its own centre, the crux. But then, as the eye moved on, the *X*, having digested the abnormalities of the *E*, sprang open once more as if to release them, simplified and consolidated, wadded and welded, as the perfect, plain, upright *I* that looked neither to the left nor the right nor straight ahead but was concerned solely with itself. The *I* was a thing apart. It was,

229

however, alongside the *T*, which was a wayside signpost, pointing both ways, a cropped cross, a headless man. Twisted within itself, EXIT had many pathways.

Robin Underleaf breathed without sound in the green glow and bowed to it, curling like a small forest animal deeper into his seat.

"Ghosts," breathed Pauline.

Nat looked beyond her pale face towards the pyramid. A thought struck him. "Perhaps the ghost has nothing to do with the tomb," he said. "What about the girl who was killed here?"

"Linda Blake."

"I'd forgotten all about her until now," he said.

"That's because you're a man."

Entwined together, they stood motionless. She turned her head away from him to listen. Only the stealth of woodland scents reached her through the gloom and she felt that she could read them. When she turned her head back to him she was part animal, part girl. She touched his lips with hers. The moisture tingled. "I like the forest," she said.

"Even though you are alone with me, in the dark, and I'm a man?"

"You mean you might kill me?"

He kissed her again, holding her head. Her neck under his hand was slender. "It would be very easy."

She had folded herself against him so that she was small. "You," she said softly. "You."

"Yes?"

"She's on your mind, that girl."

"Not her. Another girl. You."

"But you want to do the same."

"What's that?"

"Kill me."

Dr Buck Ruxton stabbed his wife on the stairs, but the hollowness of the stage so much magnified the thuds as she fell that her cries were lost. The echoes allowed Rosa Underleaf to turn loftily to her husband.

"Such a sweet girl," she murmured, with a smile in her voice. "A shame we shall see no more of her."

"Finger," he said. "Your finger."

There was an urgency in his voice that made her draw in her breath. "You make me swoon, my darling," she said, and in the darkness her hand reached to the brooch at her neck.

The maid had witnessed the murder. She, too, was on the stairs and, as Dr Ruxton climbed towards her, Rosa Underleaf's hand curled around the brooch at her neck until she felt the tip of its pin against her skin.

The doctor's knife, for the second time, rose and fell. Rosa pressed until the point punctured her fingertip. As the bloody knife dropped from the doctor's hand, Rosa's hand lay limply in her lap. The doctor began to drag the corpses to the place where he would dismember them, and Robin

Underleaf lifted his wife's hand from her lap, put her finger to his lips and sucked.

Nat took from his pocket the little phial that Robin Underleaf had given him.

"What the devil's in this?" he said.

"It's harmless," she said. "He's a nice little man."

"A nasty little man."

"But not dangerous. There's nothing dangerous in that bottle."

"No?" He held it at arm's length as she reached for it.

"I'm more dangerous than that. Give it to me."

"It's warm."

"Is it?"

"It has an internal heat."

"So have I." She pulled his head towards her. "Give it to me. It's mine."

"How do you know?"

"I know. Give it to me."

"He told me I was to give it to no one," he said. She was kissing him, reaching all the time for the bottle. "Except..."

"Except who? Stop teasing me."

"That's what you've been doing to me all evening."

For answer she pressed herself more closely to him. "Give me the bottle," she said, "and I promise." Her promise was in the way she held herself to him and she felt him weakening. "Give."

* * *

Rosa and Robin Underleaf sat together in the dark. The clock face above the green EXIT sign also glowed. It showed two minutes to midnight. Robin sucked her finger.

"Oh, hubby," she whispered, leaning her forehead on his, "isn't this exciting!"

He murmured, but he was rough and brought a twinge to her finger joint.

"Now then, my precious," she scolded, "not too hard."

On stage, Dr Buck Ruxton lumpily hauled the corpses of his wife and maidservant to the bathroom, and wailed, "The blood! The blood! It's on the stairs! The carpet is soaked!"

Rosa, enraptured, found it charming, and said so. Robin nuzzled.

"Give me the bottle," Pauline demanded.

Nat withheld it. "You wouldn't know what to do." He had pleasure in teasing. "Robin gave me instructions."

"Robin?" she said. "Are you sure it wasn't his wife?"

"His wife?"

"Old gooey-eyes," said Pauline. "You know who I mean, Rosa the man-eater."

Even by starlight he saw the distaste on her face. "Crude," he said. "That's crude."

Anger made blood rush to Pauline's cheeks, and pain drained it away just as suddenly. She had let him hold her as nobody ever before, and in the

233

night she had told him many things. And for that she was crude. "I've seen her look at you," she said.

"Oh." He stood back, raising his chin. "Am I to blame for the way someone looks at me?"

Weariness swept over her. She had been foolish to allow herself to believe that he felt as she did. He went wherever his desires took him.

"Rosa Underleaf has been good to us," he said. "She deserves better than that."

"Be careful you don't upset her." She spoke under her breath. "You might get the sack."

"What's that?" He had not heard her. "What did you say?"

"It doesn't matter."

"What did you say!"

She let her silence answer for her. She knew she had injured his pride, and she began to move towards him, but the coldness of his voice held her back.

"If that's the way you feel," he said, "so be it." He felt the thin pain of pleasure in hurting her.

She made no move to cling to him or plead. She simply stood in the forest clearing and waited.

He regarded her. She was docile, and his wish to injure her fed on her dull, unsubtle silence.

"We came here for a purpose," he said.

"Oh, yes," she said, "let's not forget that." Her sarcasm again touched the nerve of his self-esteem.

"What do you mean?" he said.

"We must not let Rosa down."

He drew in his breath and for a moment she thought he was going to strike her. She allowed only her eyes to flinch, but in place of a blow he spun away from her.

She watched him cross to the triangle of the dark pyramid. What he was about to do was trivial, a cheap excuse for walking away from her. How diminished he looked; and how small her feelings for him really were.

"Is it midnight?" he called.

"I expect so." She kept all interest from her voice, knowing now how to provoke his anger.

He was levering the stopper from the little bottle, and his fingernail bent back with a clean and exquisite pain that laid open his fury.

"Damn it all to bloody hell!"

His cry coincided with the clatter as he hurled the little bottle through the grating on to the leaf-strewn dust of the pyramid floor.

Gilray woke with a start. He listened, but the forest was silent. Nevertheless he stood up and reached for his stick.

Nat heard the bottle fracture on the floor of the tomb and waited. The dead leaves by the grating gyrated, stirred by an eddy of air and his hand was stroked by it. Then the whirlpool died. He saw nothing, and nothing clouded the space between him and Pauline. The grass did not so much as bend.

Pauline felt the chill of the night stroke her bare arm. She started back, but her arm had stiffened as if the cold air gripped it. She rubbed it, and gradually the cramp eased, but her flesh was numb. She looked down. Her skin was so soft she could barely feel it. It slid under her fingers as if it hung loose. And then she saw that it wrinkled under her hand and the wrinkles absorbed the starlight so that the whiteness of her hand and wrist had become grey. Her skin was a thin sleeve over the bone of her arm.

Gilray felt the roughness of the bark beneath his fingers, but the stick had gone. He turned and saw that another hand had grasped it.

Nat went towards Pauline. Fear had made her eyes so large that they gaped at the night. She seemed so small and so afraid, like a child, that his arrogance fell away and he became tender. He had never meant to harm her.

"Pauline," he said softly, "it's all over; the nonsense is done."

He put his arm around her shoulder and felt her subside against his breast. She did not answer.

Gilray's wail woke Wheatley. He heard Cassandra cough. Within the stick she had never felt heat nor cold, and had never been aware of breathing, but now she shivered and something caught at her throat.

The stick was lifted, and whatever it was that had made Cassandra cough now made her retch. A stench of such deep corruption, of such rot and graveyard foulness, invaded her mouth and throat that she choked. She fought to breathe, but her heavings were drowned in a tide of corpse gas.

Nat held Pauline close, and felt her head rest on his arm. Not only her eyes were wide. Her mouth was wide also.

Gilray snatched at the hand that clutched the stick but did no more than brush against the ragged and stinking sleeve as the stick was smashed against a branch. The stick jarred and fractured, and a fragment of broken machinery spun against the sky, sparkled and went out.

Nat looked down at Pauline. She rested her full weight against him, yet she was no heavier than a cloak across his arm. To rouse her, he said her name. And then again, leaning closer. Her mouth, as empty as the sockets of her eyes, sagged wide as if she screamed, but no sound came.

Arms held as high as a Spanish dancer, Rosa forced her way through the crowd. "A truly wonderful evening!" she cried. "Everything went so well, don't you think? Super! Super!"

Nat saw the hank of hair, and the bone beneath the

237

skin. The whole glade, open to the sky, was not wide enough to contain the cry he sent against the stars.

33

CASSANDRA

Nat lifted Pauline. She was almost weightless, so light that he was able to run with her in his arms away from the pyramid and along the forest track.

He was putting Pauline in the car when Cassandra opened her eyes. She saw the pale glimmer of whitewashed walls and the scanty sparks of stars through the grime of a glass roof, and she remembered where she was. She also knew what she had done.

Wheatley came to his senses lying against a wall. As the stick shattered, the shock must have thrown him there. Then he, too, saw the stars through the roof and knew it had all happened while he slept. But now he was awake and the dream was over.

It was Cassandra who remembered what they had truly done. "What a place for it to happen," she murmured, and she moved her hands across the bare floorboards seeking Wheatley. He wasn't there.

What troubled Wheatley, now that he was fully awake, was not the dream but that he had no recollection of what he had done to bring himself to be lying in the dark on a wooden floor. He eased himself up until he was on all fours. He remembered a sensation of tumbling through the air under the stars. What had he been up to?

"Oh hell!" he moaned.

There was a cool, musty smell. Whitewash. Thank God for that. The stench of something much worse lingered in his nostrils, and the recollection of a figure striding from a tomb. But that was only the nightmare. He cleared his lungs and, because the sound of his own voice reassured him, he spoke aloud to himself. "I must have passed out," he said, and was startled when, from somewhere nearby, another voice answered.

"Bob? Is that you?"

He crawled across the floor to where Cassandra lay. "Did we try to ride that damned bike in here, and fall off?" he said. "How long have we been out – it's dark."

"Bob," she said. "Don't you remember?"

He was troubled by hearing a schoolgirl whispering his name in the dark. "Who said you could call me that?"

"No one." She kissed him, and the soft touch of her lips teased from deep within his mind memories he had hoped were false. "What have I done?" he said.

"What have *we* done, you mean." She still held him close, and he groaned. "Don't you like it?"

There was confidence in her voice, so much certainty that he knew she must have some hold over him. He spoke cautiously, trying to sort reality from a jumble of sensations, some of which belonged to sleep. "Twice," he said. "Twice Gilray has tricked me, hypnotized me somehow."

"Me, too," she said.

"But none of it is true, Cassandra. None of it."

She was silent for a moment. "Some of it is," she said softly.

Her confidence made him fearful. "I don't know what you mean."

For answer, her lips touched him again.

"Don't, Cassandra," he said.

"You weren't afraid of me a little while ago," she whispered, "in the forest."

"We were never in a forest. We have never been out of this room."

"Maybe you're right." She was quite untroubled, content to agree. "Maybe it all happened here."

For long moments he was silent. Then he asked, "We didn't, did we?"

"We did."

She had already considered what would come of it, but did not tell him all she knew. "Don't worry," she said.

34

Nat sat in the hospital corridor. The brightness of the lights threw almost no shadows, and people seemed to swim past him with as little effort as it had taken him to carry Pauline to the car.

The night passed. He had to answer many questions, and his parents, against his will, were called as well as Pauline's, but at dawn he returned to the casualty ward and was allowed to see her alone. The drained and empty horror he thought he had seen in the starlight was, in the hospital bed, a girl again, but pale and thin. Her constitution, they said, could never have been strong, and some collapse like this had always been likely. They insisted that he himself was not to blame. He paid no heed to what they said.

When, in the days that followed, Pauline's mother came to see her, she brought with her a pall of anxiety. "Your father can't come," she said, "you know how he is with hospitals." Her drab coat, which she never removed, and the straggle of her wild hair advertised a trouble that pleaded for more attention than was being given to her daughter, and it was not difficult for Nat to persuade her to leave. Pauline lay pale on her pillow, and Nat kept watch.

Cassandra came and held her hand, and when Pauline gained strength the two girls would talk long and secretly.

As the days went by Nat guarded her more jealously. Once, when he found his father at her bedside with a prayer book in his hand he drove him out with such cold disdain his father thought it best not to return, and when his mother spoke of a "caring relationship" going too far he put his foot through her guitar.

It was Nat who brought Pauline out of the shadow of the pyramid.

Before she was due to go back to school, they walked through the town and talked about Cassandra. On the riverbank the flowers had gone, and the autumn grass was bent over, waiting for winter.

"That's where she told me about him," said Pauline. "But not his name."

"Didn't you guess?"

She laughed. "How could I? They kept it so secret."

"It's too big to be a secret any longer."

Pauline smiled. "And nobody knows where

243

they are now," she said.

"Except you."

"Except me."

Nat put his arm around her. "And that leaves us," he said. She nodded and rested her head on his shoulder. That night she died.

35

"Sir," he said, "you seem to have frequented the
schools. What sciences did you study?"

"Knight errantry," replied Don Quixote, "which
is as good as poetry, and even two inches better."

– Cervantes, *Don Quixote*

A dull day in October, and the grey light that
filtered into the bar of The Golden Lion was so
meagre that even early in the afternoon the fire
made shadows flicker on the walls. Nat, gazing
into the flames, did not look up when the door into
the alleyway opened and slow footsteps shuffled
over the flags. The landlord came out of the back
room.

There was a muffled exchange of words at the
bar, and Nat lifted his pint of Three Corners and
squinted at the flames dancing within the glass. He
did not listen to what was being said. He rarely
listened to anything. Pauline had been dead for five
weeks. He had never once been back to the shop.

No one had ever spoken to him about the ghost hunting. It did not matter.

The landlord's voice, only slightly louder, took on authority. "You can turn yourself around and go right out again."

Nat looked over his shoulder. A figure at the bar had turned away and was obediently making its way to the door. The landlord caught Nat's eye. "A few more like him," he said, "and I'll be out of business."

The figure, hunched in a dirty overcoat, glanced guiltily at Nat. It was a man twice, three times, his age and ashamed of being poor. Nat looked away. Who hadn't got problems? He yawned.

"And take this with you." The landlord picked up a hat from the bar and skimmed it after the man. It curved away and fell near Nat. He picked it up. "I'll buy him a drink," he said.

"That you won't," said the landlord.

"I can pay."

"Makes no difference here, son."

"Why not?"

"Because I bloody say so."

The landlord rested closed fists on the bar, one each side of the pumps. His shirtsleeves were rolled in a tight ring around the muscles of his forearms, and his dewy brown eyes bulged with the desire to do damage.

"Sorry to be a nuisance," the man murmured, reaching for his hat. "Please don't perturb yourself."

"OK," said Nat. "OK." There was no need to argue with the landlord. No need to take risks. No need to do anything except think of Pauline. So he emptied his glass before he handed the man his hat and stood up.

They had never met, yet the man smiled as if they knew each other.

"This is a lousy pub, anyway." Nat did not look at the landlord, but intended that he should hear.

The man was courteously standing back to allow Nat to go out first when the flap of the bar counter was flung up and the landlord, lusting to lay hands on an arrogant schoolboy and a snivelling tramp, came for them. Nat cringed and turned with his hands up to protect his head. He saw that the tramp, a small man, stood in the landlord's path.

"Hey!" Nat cried out to bring his courage back, and he put out a hand to grab at the tramp and pull him away.

It was not necessary. The browbeaten little man seemed suddenly to gain height, so that he was face to face with the brown bullock-gaze. The landlord, taken by surprise, stopped. For a full two seconds the tramp gazed him down before he seemed to regain his proper height. Then he turned his back on the landlord and shepherded Nat out ahead of him.

"How come?" said Nat, once they had reached the alleyway.

"Beg pardon?" Apprehensive eyes looked up

from under the brim of the greasy hat, and Nat realized with a shock where they had seen each other once before. At Pauline's funeral. He had been the stranger at the edge of the mourners, his plump face so ugly with grief that Nat had resented him. He had had no right to be so full of sorrow when the loss was Nat's alone.

"How come you stopped him chucking us out?" Nat did not try to keep the antagonism out of his voice.

The hunched shoulders lifted in a shrug.

"You suddenly seemed two foot taller." Nat was impatient. "Either that, or you came off the ground."

"Did I?" The hat was pushed back and he rubbed his fingertips across a bald forehead. "Did I?" Then the grubby plumpness of his cheeks was pushed about by a grin. "Maybe I did."

Nat, dismissing him, turned to his bike, which he had left leaning against the pub wall. "See you around," he said.

"You did not lock it?"

"This?" Nat rattled the machine. "Who'd want to nick this load of junk?"

"Dearie, dearie me." The man tutted and shook his head. "What a neglectful person you are, Mr..." Nat, in no mood for politeness, did not give his name. Unperturbed, the stranger went on. "You were most courteous to me a moment ago and proffered drink to this shabby personage. May I be permitted to return the compliment?"

"I'm not going back in there. Don't you think it."

The little man's lips pursed as if he was about to whistle but only to issue an eightsome string of denials. "No-no-no-no-no-no-no-no! But I can do wonders for the pitiful machinery under your hand."

36

But when the fields are still,
And the tired men and dogs all gone to rest,
And only the white sheep are sometimes seen
Cross and recross the strips of moon-blanch'd
*   green,*
Come, shepherd, and again begin the quest!
                    – Matthew Arnold, *The Scholar-Gipsy*

Nat looked up at the glass roof. "I didn't know this place existed," he said.

"Few persons do." Gilray had lifted Nat's bicycle and it swung between them on long chains. "I am only in a titchy way of business. Machinery does not come my way so often. I do not look for it, not since…" He broke off and gazed through the cycle frame with such a depth of sadness in his plump, pale face that Nat's suspicion of him turned to pity. "But it is gladness to perform small service for friend."

Gilray's sudden smile took Nat by surprise and

he found himself saying, "We met once before … almost met, I mean." And then he wished he had said nothing, for the little man was puzzled.

"Forgive discourtesy," said Gilray, "but I do not remember." Then he seemed to recognize that Nat was unwilling to speak, for he busied himself with the machine as though he expected no reply.

Nat watched him as he renewed the neglected machine. Gilray worked without removing his overcoat, but all his clothing was so shabby that extra grubbiness hardly seemed to matter. But there was pleasure in watching the clever work of his fingers, and the small sounds he made were absorbed so completely by the large silence of the big room that some of the pain in Nat's mind eased.

"I saw you at a funeral," he said. "She was a girl." When he gave Pauline's name to Gilray he realized that it was the first time he had spoken it aloud since she died. "Did you know her?" he asked.

"Alas." Gilray had taken off his hat and pressed it to his chest. "I did not know her. All I know was that she was too young to die."

He searched Nat's face as if yearning to show how deeply he shared his grief, but Nat could not hold his eyes and only the gentle tap of a chain touching the cycle frame broke the silence until Gilray said softly, "Now I understand your downcast visage, young sir, but I also have had my time of turmoil."

Nat's frown made it plain he did not wish to hear

of other people's troubles, but Gilray did not fall silent. "I was in great torment," he said. "I had made a mistake which plagued my mind – deeply, deeply twisted in my brain." He made a gesture with the hand holding his hat as if he wished to brush away the memory.

Nat was brutal. He saw the anguish on Gilray's face but he asked, "What mistake?"

Gilray avoided his eyes. Nat said nothing, allowing the silence to ask the question, and after a long moment Gilray said, "I came across a person I suspected of great beastliness. He could harm young persons, I was certain sure, and I did not do enough…"

He broke off, as if disgusted with himself, but after a while he resumed. "I did truly believe I had acted to make all safe, but I did not do enough! I thought I had brought an end to beastliness, but I had not. And then when I heard tell of so young a maid as your Miss Pauline so cruelly struck down my head did churn with wild alarm. I feared she had been a victim of the awfulness."

Nat cut across him. "No one attacked her," he said. "I was with her all the time."

"Please not to be angry," Gilray pleaded. "I was mistaken about her danger. She did not suffer the fate I feared – I do not believe she was ever near the place where it could take place. I was a person of silly whims." He attempted to smile. "And she had a good protector – a stalwart brave young fellow-me-lad, as I well do know."

In the foyer of the museum Fred Wherry lifted the glass lid of the case that held the bound copies of *The Messenger* and held it open with his head while he turned the page. "I had someone enquiring about your friend Wheatley this morning," he said.

Peg was behind the counter of the cash desk putting new booklets in the racks. "I don't know why you insist on saying *my* friend – he was yours, too."

"Friend Wheatley's only interest was in females, or hadn't you noticed?" He was looking at her through the glass frame that rested against his forehead.

"You look like a bloody goldfish," she said.

"Oho-oho." His coy complacency maddened her even more. "I seem to have hit a sore point."

Beneath the counter she screwed up a handful of the new leaflets he'd had printed. "Who," she asked carefully, "was asking after Bob Wheatley?"

"That fat little bozo – the one who was always eyeballing the esoteric documentation we have here." Wherry had put on one of his "voices", knowing it grated.

"Do you mean Mr Gilray?" she asked primly.

"Uh-hu."

"What did you tell him?"

"I told him zilch."

"I hope you weren't unfriendly. He's a nice little man."

Wherry did not enlighten her. He closed the lid. "Personally," he said, "I'm glad we've seen the last of Bob Wheatley. It was always on the cards he would blot his copybook in the way he has."

"I hope," said Peg, "they are very happy together. There's no reason why they shouldn't be. He's nice, is Bob. And she's a lucky girl."

Wherry locked the case. He stood for a moment, putting his two index fingers on the edges of the polished wood and then sliding them apart and around the frame with smug precision as if demonstrating a theorem that only he had perceived. Behind the counter, Peg scrubbed her foot on the pamphlets. Wherry said, "And we shan't be seeing Mr Gilray any more, either."

"Why not?"

"He has deteriorated." Wherry's pale eyes were on her, judging her reaction. "His appearance is disgraceful. I shooed him away and made it clear he was no longer welcome. He won't be back."

Peg did not give him the pleasure of letting him see what she felt, but later in the day, when the nice-looking boy who used to be one of Bob Wheatley's pupils came in, she took her revenge.

Gilray would not take any payment for repairing Nat's bicycle. In the whitewashed room the battered machine soon gleamed with so many new parts that when Gilray, suddenly blushing, asked Nat a favour he could not refuse.

It was only an errand. "I do some trivial,

254

itty-bitty delvings into matters long past and gone," Gilray said, and he laughed shyly when he told Nat that he had wished to visit the museum but they did not approve of his tramp-like appearance. Yet all he had wanted was to consult a certain book to be found only there: a diary in manuscript.

"You, young master, a respected scholarly young chappie, all neat and clean, will gain access." And then he sniggered, broken-toothed and pitiful, "Be you my Trojan Horse, I pray."

It was late in the afternoon when Nat climbed the steps to the museum's door. There was no one at the counter in the foyer, and when he went through the archway into the galleries all was quiet, no visitors to be seen. He knocked at the door of the office but there was no reply.

He was walking back across the foyer and looking out through the glass panels of the main door into the square outside where the street lamps were already lighting the deserted pavements when the thought entered his mind that perhaps he could borrow the book without troubling the curator. No one had seen him enter, and there was at present no one outside to see him leave. It would take but a moment to pocket the book and be gone.

Nat ceased to breathe. He turned quietly and, taking short steps so that the soft soles of his shoes did not squeak on the polished floor, he crossed to the deep alcove of the library entrance. He paused in its shadow, already a thief, grasped the large, cold handle of the door, turned it and felt the smooth withdrawal of the catch. He pushed, and the heavy old door moved inwards without a sound. It was an invitation. He stepped through and closed the door behind him.

Even the lights were on in the long room, as if the library welcomed what he was doing. But the lights also meant it was likely that there was someone in one of the bays made by the shelves that jutted out on either side.

"Hello." Nat pitched his voice just high enough to be heard. "Is there anyone there?"

There was no response, and he went forward quietly but humming innocently and looking from left to right into each bay as he came to it, but all were empty. At the far end of the room his breathing, which he had forced to become easier, tightened once more as he saw that the lower shelves were protected by brass lattice-work, and the cupboards beneath had heavy handles and escutcheons. Gilray had told him where the manuscripts were kept but had failed to mention that the cupboards could be locked.

Nat stooped to the centre cupboard and reached for the handle. Anyone seeing him now would take him for a thief, but he owed it to Gilray to try. If the cupboard stayed closed he would walk out. He pulled gently and the door did not budge. He was about to turn his back and leave when his hand, as if acting in defiance of himself, gave the handle another turn and with a soft click the door swung open. Now he was honour-bound to become a thief, and his heart pounded. He crouched and began to search.

There were a number of books and papers on the shelf but the diary was easy to pick out. He lifted it and was turning its pages when the lights at the far end of the room went out. His heart jolted and he jerked his head around at the same instant as a little cry of surprise came from the shadows of the doorway.

Nat got to his feet and stood rigidly still. The figure at the door was indistinct, but then a woman's voice reached him.

"I didn't see you. Nobody told me there was anybody here."

Nat put the book onto a library desk. His voice caught and he had to begin twice. "I was just looking," he said, and added, "for something."

The voice was suspicious. "Have you permission?"

Nat shook his head. "I didn't know I needed it."

The woman came into the light. "Didn't know?" she said. She was small and quite plump. He might, in other circumstances, have liked her, but she had moral authority over him. "Why don't you know? You've been here before. I've seen you."

"I just thought," he said, and had to swallow. "I thought, as there was no one around, that I could look something up." He felt slackness in his limbs and would have liked to sit down. Or walk out. "Sorry," he said. "I'll go."

"Hold on." She put up a hand ordering him not to move. "I do know you. What's your name?"

He had to tell her, feeling like a child, and he struggled to keep something like confidence in his voice.

"Ah," she said, nodding, "and you needn't be so truculent. Why are you here?"

"My teacher." It was a sudden lie. "I was looking up something for Mr Wheatley." She had begun to smile, but now her expression changed. "I was doing it for him," he said.

"Oh, no you weren't." The light from above was harsh on her. The friendliness had left her face. "Bob Wheatley isn't here any more. He's gone."

She had changed so suddenly that he was cautious. He nodded.

"So don't give me any nonsense about Bob Wheatley sending you here. He's gone off with his silly little tart of a girlfriend."

"No!" Nat's reaction surprised them both. He found himself staring at her and panting, and suddenly he was afraid that she might mistake his reaction for anger and become alarmed. He lowered his voice. "She's not what you say she is. I think you're wrong about her."

It was now that he would be thrown out of the library, everything lost. He moved as if to walk past her.

"Wait a minute." Her head drooped as she considered what to do about him. "So you know the girl ..." she corrected herself "... used to know her. Knew her well?"

"Yes. Cassandra Ashe."

She took a long time to answer, and he knew what was in her mind even before she raised her eyes to him and her face softened. She thought he was a boy who had loved Cassandra and had been let down.

"Nat Woodburn," she said, "I apologize." Her eyes sought his face and rested on him with such intensity that he saw she was willing him to understand something else, something about herself. "You're not alone," she said. "I know how you feel." She gave him a small, twisted smile so that he should know what she meant. He had lost Cassandra, but she had lost Wheatley.

"I'm sorry," he said.

"Don't worry about it." Again she regarded him so long and steadily that he had to look away. "Well, they've gone," she said, "both of them." There was so much sympathy in her voice that he did not let her know that Cassandra was nothing to him. "Do you know where they are now?" she asked.

"No." He spoke to the floor. "They've gone for good." It was Pauline who would never come back, but he would not say so.

Peg Wherry drew a deep breath and became businesslike. "So why are you here in this library, Nat Woodburn?"

He began to tell her. "There's a diary by a

259

doctor…" but she flung up her hands.

"Not another one!" she cried. "Why all this interest? And why you, Nat?"

She had dropped his surname. Now he owed her some honesty. "It's not for me alone," he said. "Someone else wants it. Badly."

"Aren't you going to tell me who?" She was coaxing him, half-smiling.

"Someone who is very interested."

"Stop teasing me, Nat. I want to know."

"Oh, well." He sighed. "You might as well know before you throw me out." He watched to see her reaction. "His name's Gilray … and he's already been told not to come here."

She closed her lips and gave a little grunt down her nose. "I might have known."

"So I'll be off, if that's all right with you."

"Hold on." She put out a hand. "What's his interest?"

"You wouldn't believe it if I told you."

"Try me." She was smiling, letting him know she knew more than she was telling.

"It's something about the supernatural. It's research. Look," he said, "why don't you just let me go and forget all about it."

"Your Mr Gilray," she said, "I've seen him around. He's harmless, isn't he?"

"Oh, yes he is," Nat agreed. "Very."

"Easily hurt?"

"I think so."

She swept suddenly past him, picked up the

diary from the desk, thrust it into Nat's hand, turned him around and began to push him to the door. "Give it to him," she said, "with my compliments." He began to protest. "Go!" she ordered.

37

He who wrote what I hold in my hand,
  Centuries back was so good as to die,
Leaving this rubbish to cumber the land.
    – Robert Browning, *Sibrandus Schafnaburgensis*

"Ta muchly," said Gilray and put the diary in his raglan pocket.

"She practically threw it at me," said Nat, "as if she didn't want to see it again."

"It shall be preserved for future times, never fear."

They were walking, an odd couple, through the centre of town as day began to fade. Gilray, head bent, shuffled at the kerbside and Nat, much taller, dawdled to keep pace with him.

"What is in it that should cause so much trouble?" Nat asked. "It's only a book."

"So's the Bible, mon ami."

"Quite." Nat was impatient at being taken for a fool. He had glanced through the diary and knew what it was. "But this is the maunderings of an old crackpot – as I know for a fact."

"How so?" Gilray's interest seemed suddenly sharp.

"I know a bit about Doctor Carr and his pyramid, that's all. He doesn't amount to much." He could not speak of fruitless ghost-hunting without mentioning Pauline again. "All I know is that magic doesn't work."

"Some believe." They had reached the tunnel leading to the alleyway and Gilray turned into it. "Some persons..." he began but the rest of his mumble was lost as he went ahead.

The coldness of the alleyway was not as bleak as the chill that closed in on them within the workshop. Whatever light was left in the dying day was concentrated under the glass roof, but already the white walls were washed with grey. The night would be soundless here, and Gilray, sleeping beneath the bench in the corner, would be known to no one. It was a deeper loneliness than even Nat felt.

Any words said in this space took on strange meanings, so that Nat was not embarrassed to speak seriously of matters that elsewhere would have been eccentric. "Is the diary a dangerous book?" he asked.

"All books..." Gilray began, and then he saw that Nat was accepting no platitudes. "It *is* somewhat dangerous," he said.

"In itself?" Nat insisted. "I'm not talking about

its effect on people's minds – all books do something to people."

Gilray took the diary from his pocket and laid it on the bench. "In itself? You mean by merely touching it I am tarnished?" He paused and then, just before Nat was about to speak, he said, "It is perhaps the key to a mystery, that is its danger."

The diary was brief, and Nat had read it through. "What mystery?" he asked.

"The diary is nothing," said Gilray. "All his vileness is in another book. All his venom is wound up in spells and written down."

"Yes," said Nat, "his grimoire; you told me." He was losing patience.

"It is lost to us!" Gilray's anguish flared again. "It must be found for it leaks harmfulness here and everywhere." He patted the pages of the diary. "This could unlock its hiding place."

"But you have already looked through it and found nothing."

"We need to search again. We have nothing else."

Nat breathed deeply in order to hide a sigh. "Well, I've read it, as you asked me," he said, "but I found no mention of a grimoire."

"Not even hidden?" Gilray spoke keenly. "I told you to hunt for *G* – any *G* standing alone may lead us there; it was his manner to write in formulae and be devious."

"No *G*, nor grimoire written out in full. Nor has anyone else as far as I know. People have read this stuff again and again and found nothing, isn't that so?"

Gilray dipped his head and gave out a moan so like a frightened child that Nat, to comfort him, said, "There's no need to worry; no harm can be done. It's quite impossible for spells to work."

Gilray's head jerked up so violently that his hat fell off. He was bald and had a baby face. It would have been laughable to see him like this except that, with his head flung back, his nostrils were pointed forward like a bat's and his voice rose to a squeal. "A girl died! Did you hear me what I say! A young lady did die!"

The outburst was so grotesque that Nat drew back, but he conquered his distaste and said plainly, "That was nothing to do with why she died." Nothing would make him admit that what had happened to Pauline was in the slightest way connected with the tomb or what they had done there. "It didn't come to anything. Nothing happened."

But Gilray's voice rose once more. "He killed her! She lay dead near the tomb!"

And then Nat saw he had been mistaken. What Gilray was saying had nothing to do with Pauline. Gilray was speaking of the girl who was murdered by her heavy-fisted lover. Linda Blake. He held up a hand to quieten the little man. "I thought you were talking about…" He wanted to leave it there, hanging in the air, but a sudden sharp tilt of the baby face showed that Gilray had detected something and needed to be told more. "I didn't know you were thinking about Linda Blake," Nat said. "I thought you meant someone else."

"Who? Who did you think?"

Again Nat paused. "I thought you meant the girl I knew." He drew in his breath before he said her name. "Pauline. We were there, at the tomb, not long before she died."

The anger drained from Gilray. His face softened and Nat was lowering his own eyes, acknowledging Gilray's sympathy, when he saw it was not sadness that had changed Gilray's expression. His small mouth hung open and his eyes were wide because he was in the grip of what appeared to be horror. When at length, having run his tongue over his lips, he spoke again his voice was barely audible. "Why," he said, "why were you at the tomb? What did you do?"

"We were there when she was first taken ill. There's nothing more to it than that, Mr Gilray."

But Gilray leant forward, and the intensity of his gaze showed his distrust of what he was being told. "What did you do?" It was a command. "Tell me what you did at the pyramid!"

"It was nothing. It was foolishness. We were ghost-hunting."

"What did you do!" The ferocity in the little man made Nat resent his question.

"Nothing. Nothing at all – I just had to be there with a girl, that's all."

"*Had* to be? Why *had*? Who said *had*!"

266

Nat blew out his cheeks. "Well, if you want to know all that, it was to please Robin Underleaf at the bookshop. And his wife, if you must know every detail. They're a couple of cranks, but I followed their instructions. It wasn't anything sensible."

There was a long silence during which Gilray did not once look in Nat's direction. When he spoke, it was to the empty space under the glass roof, and the gathering dimness all but swallowed his voice. "The servants," he said. "I have found the servants. While I looked elsewhere they sent their innocents to the tomb."

"We came away," said Nat. "I brought her away. Nothing happened."

Gilray's eyes were lost in shadow. He began to moan and when words came they were a wail of pain. "Mea culpa! Mea culpa! Nat, my brother, I am to blame. I did not see. I was blind. They used you. They damaged her."

"How damaged? What do you mean damaged? She was ill – it could have happened at any time." Nat shook his head. "Don't try to make me believe anything else. It was all nonsense – a bit of stupid ceremonial to bring out a ghost who did not appear."

Gilray's face was ashen, but his voice was firm. "Monsieur and Madame Underleaf did not believe it nonsense. They were afraid of what they meddled in, so they sent you in their place." He thrust his head forward. "They put *you* in danger!"

267

Nat drew back. "You're not trying to tell me that they are responsible for anything that happened to Pauline."

Gilray was bent over the diary. "I say nothing."

"Then tell me what you're doing? Why do you want to find a book of spells?"

"Those who believe in evil create evil. There is badness there."

"But it's just the nonsense of a pair of fools. Even they know it doesn't work, they've never even tried to see me to find out what happened."

"Oh!" As if a great pain had gripped him, Gilray groaned and put both hands to his head. "Oh, Nat, it is worse than I feared!"

Exasperated almost beyond endurance, Nat said, "But it's just madness. It has to be!"

Gilray did not attempt to deny it. He had become calm. "Foolish or not," he said, "they are servants of the pyramid. The servants fear their Master, and their Master has the key to the greatest secrets. I must search."

Nat opened his mouth to speak, but Gilray waved a hand to keep him silent, and bent again to the diary.

38

---

*Everlasting Reliques: In old magic
I retain grasp.*

— Doctor Septimus Carr

Nat waited. He believed nothing that Gilray believed, but something he himself had said made him linger in the cold room where the light faded more and more rapidly and the only sound was the faint rustle as Gilray searched the diary of Doctor Septimus Carr for answers to unanswerable questions. Nat dismissed it all, but there was one question that could be answered, and he should have asked it before now. Why had Rosa and Robin Underleaf never once attempted to discover from him what had happened at the pyramid?

Closer and closer to the pages went Gilray's nose as he raced the dwindling daylight, and then, when shadows had lapped in like the tide and swamped him, he laid the book on the bench and raised his head. "Nothing," he said. "There is nothing."

The words came as a relief to Nat. If there was nothing in the book, there was nothing in his own question. There was no need now to wonder why the Underleafs had never approached him; they had been ashamed to do so because their experiment, far from being a success, had resulted in nothing. There was no difference between them and the fake magician of long ago. And Gilray was another dupe and, Nat realized, he had himself been in danger of being infected by it. It was time to go.

Gilray saw him stir. "Hungered?" he said. "Dost thou wish to eat?"

Nat glanced around. He realized he did not know where or what Gilray ate. There was not, as far as he knew, anything like a kitchen in the building, and he had never seen any sign of food.

"You mistake me, Nat. Pastrycook I was, pastrycook I shall be, but in this present now I am nothing. Buy bread we must."

It was to humour him that Nat walked with him through town. They crossed the bridge. The wind, sweeping in from the fens, planed the wavelets smooth on the brown river and tested its sharpness on their cheeks. Gilray walked with a slow shuffle, and Nat saw that the sole of one of his shoes was coming off.

"Where are we going?" he asked. They had turned onto the quayside, and they could already see the last street lamps glimmering against the night clouds which heaped their darkness on the fields beyond the town.

Nat knew of nowhere they could eat, but Gilray said, "Fine little place hereabouts." He had his head bent against the wind that hissed as it swept wisps of straw and grit along the empty quay. At this point the bank was built up to keep the river at high tide from washing through the town, and at the foot of the bank a row of small houses sheltered like wintering snails. One was a baker's shop into which Gilray disappeared, leaving Nat outside.

Through the window he watched Gilray giving his order to a fat woman with frizzed hair, and he was about to turn away when his eye was caught by the sloping nameboard that ran along the window's bottom edge. It was blank. Whatever name it had once borne had been painted over many times, but the raking light from inside the shop showed up the shadows of the buried lettering of long ago. With nothing better to do he leant forward to read it, but at that moment the shopkeeper reached under the transparent plastic sheeting that already covered her trays of cakes for the night. Her broad shadow obliterated the lettering and from under her mass of hair she gave Nat an aggressive glare. He turned away, mildly intrigued at the initials he thought he had seen, but when Gilray joined him, looking cold and wan, it was too trivial to mention.

They walked back along the riverbank. Street lamps were coming on, polishing the brown water to make it gleam, and for a moment Nat's spirits lifted, but then they turned their backs on the glitter of the river and found their way to the emptiness of the workshop. By day it suited Nat's mood; it was as hollow and featureless as his days had become, but at night it was a cell, and to be there in the pallid dimness under the glass roof was proof that he was losing his self-esteem just as surely as Gilray had lost his. Then, on the bench under which Gilray slept, a Tilley lamp hissed and was lifted to a hook above them.

"We shall have a repast," said Gilray, and he took from his pocket the food he had bought. He tore open a paper bag and held a sausage roll into the glare of the lamp. He prodded it. "The hardness is magnificent." He broke it in two. "The flakiness of the pastry has a dull heaviness which makes its glueiness adhere to the teeth." He was enraptured. "And the meat, young sir, just look at the pinkness of it! Far, far from natural – only an artificial tincture could possibly bring such a fever to the product." He sniffed it. "Preservatives," he said. "And such a glutinous solidity, such a heaviness that I wonder at it!"

Gilray gestured towards what lay spread out on the torn paper. "Partake where you will."

Nat picked up another sausage roll.

"A meal in itself," said Gilray.

Nat bit. "Very doughy," he said.

"You are a connoisseur," said Gilray.

For a while Nat ate. Then he paused and said,

"I thought I saw something a bit odd at the baker's shop."

"Of interest, I hope?"

"I thought I saw a name, or part of a name, that had been painted over. It began with a *G*."

They sat on the bench, one at either end, with the food spread out between them and the harsh whiteness of the lamp casting its cone of light from above. Gilray had pushed his hat to the back of his head so that the baldness of his brow shone but nevertheless cast a shadow over his face except for the tip of his snub nose. He ate, not replying.

"I saw a *G*," said Nat. "The letter you told me to look for in the diary. Quite a coincidence."

"*G* stands for many things," said Gilray.

"For Gilray." Nat gazed steadily at him, aware that he had sloped his body in order to be within the protection of the tent made by the light. They were both leaning forward, towards each other. "I saw a bit more than the first letter... I thought the name on the baker's shop could have been Gilray."

"This sausage roll is a tasty mausoleum of deceased pig," said Gilray, "and those apple pies could only have been wrought by a master pastry-man. Observe, if you will, the cracking of the lids, and the paste of apple that seeps therefrom. A touch of genius in its sliminess." Then he looked up, and his tone altered. "You are keen, Nathaniel. I was once, in my travels up and down the years, the baker who owned the shop."

"Did she recognize you?"

"Why should she? It was many years ago."

Nat lifted his half-eaten sausage roll. "I hope you were better than this."

Gilray tilted his head so that his face was deeper in shadow. "In times of perfection," he mumbled, "imperfections are much in demand. My reputation as a master chef is founded on broken pastry and sogginess."

"This is not a time for perfection," said Nat.

"No." Gilray's voice was low. "But add a century or two to what is now, and there is a fashion for imperfect things. My broken crusts are famous in the future time."

The light from directly overhead emphasized his plump cheeks and the downward turn of his mouth, so that Nat could have been looking into the face of a pug dog. A dog-headed man. Some future breed. Nat, feeling his imagination slipping out of control, struggled to clear his head.

"Young man." Gilray's jowls shook as he spoke. "You don't know what you do, what risks you run."

Nat knew that Gilray could not be sane. It was time to break out of this tent of light where he sat with a madman, and when Gilray turned his head away he saw his chance. He was easing himself slowly upright, ready to slip from the bench, when Gilray, looking out into the darkness, suddenly called out, "Here!"

Nat's muscles seized. Gilray had an accomplice.

He was trapped. He held himself still, listening and looking.

At the far side of the room, hidden in darkness, something stirred. Gilray was also looking. There was a tap on the floorboards, and then another, but what caused the sound was invisible. Nat strained to see, and had begun to draw up his legs when he caught sight of the faint glint of an eye approaching. It was at less than man height and as it came forward the tapping, like the sound of a hoof or a claw on wood, advanced with it. Yet there was nothing visible. Nothing except a glimmer.

Nat swung to face whatever it was. He saw a black rod. It rested on the floor, but whoever wielded it was still lost in shadow. It began to move and he raised his arms to protect himself when, suddenly, it leapt clear of the ground and into Gilray's hand.

Gilray laid it on the bench between them. "Fear not," he said. "It is no more than my slim little friend – slightly the worse for wear, yet active still."

Nat took his eyes from the walking-stick to gaze out into the darkness. "Someone threw it to you," he said.

"We are alone," said Gilray.

"It's a trick. There's a spring somewhere."

Gilray nodded. "A device," he said. "Something that was made by a brain. As was a pyramid. And a book of spells." Suddenly he reached for the stick and smashed it down on the diary. "Listen!" His voice filled the room. "My stick is nothing. A mere trickle of small powers, but it rides on a knowledge that is vast. Strange routes lead to it. It makes or unmakes. As do spells."

Nat was silent. Little by little he was being persuaded to leave the real world, and he fought against what was being asked of him. The stick was clever conjuring, but now he was expected to deal with magic. "Spells," he said. "Do you really believe they have power?"

"Alas," said Gilray, and nodded.

"But how can they? Where does it come from?"

"It lies within us," said Gilray.

Nat drew in his breath. Every sermon his father gave had the same message – everything lay within us; it was the big get-out, lifting the blame from God's shoulders. "There's nothing new in saying that," he said.

"Nor does there need to be. We make our own gods, large or small. We decide."

"Give me that book," said Nat. He was careless now. He would play with spells if that's what was needed. He held out a hand and Gilray gave him the diary.

"You say there is a clue to a more dangerous book in this but you cannot find it."

Gilray nodded. "His grimoire," he said, "is hidden because it burns with terribleness."

"Then a parson's son should be just the boy to find it." Nat opened the book. "By divination," he said and stabbed at the first page. His finger, as he intended, rested on the title: "Everlasting

Reliques." He read it out, and added, "He was more than a little conceited about his memoirs, wasn't he, expecting them to last for ever?"

Gilray folded his hands in his lap and offered no comment.

Nat was about to turn the page when he noticed that, under the glare of the lamp, the words of the title had a rustiness that differed from the words below it. He became mock serious. "Hello, hello," he said, "what have we here? Could this be written in blood?"

"It is likely," said Gilray.

"Of course," said Nat, "but is it significant?"

"It is a title," said Gilray

"But there's nothing there that begins with your magic letter G, if that's what we are still searching for?" He raised his eyebrows asking the question of Gilray, who replied solemnly but without hope, "We seek the grimoire, and that is a G."

"Then I must make another stab." Nat riffled the pages, but too energetically and the diary fell open at its last page. "Damn," he said. Then "Devil," he thought, for once more, but this time at the page's foot, there were more words of a faded rustiness. "Topped and tailed in blood," he said, "and this time there is indeed a G."

"But signifying nothing," said Gilray as they both looked down on the last words of the diary and Nat read them aloud: "In old magic I retain grasp."

"The word grasp is G," said Gilray, "but has

no connection with grimoire."

Nat nodded. "And it is a careless sentence, anyway," he said. "He's missed a word out – shouldn't it read: In old magic I retain *my* grasp?"

"He was old," said Gilray. "Perhaps careless."

"Perhaps," Nat agreed, although carelessness did not seem to him to be one of Doctor Carr's failings. "For a moment I thought we were on to something." He reached out to touch the book again. "I've been from front to back, so let me go from back to front." He was about to riffle the pages once more when he paused.

"Yes?" Gilray waited for him.

"It's that missing word," said Nat. "Why is it not there, I wonder. Doctor Carr strove to get his spells right, didn't he? Why get the last sentence wrong?" He shrugged. "Oh well, now we go from back to front."

This time he did begin to turn the pages, but then he suddenly flung the book flat and pressed it open at the back page. "And why does it end with the word grasp?" His head jerked forward and he began to run his finger under the words, beginning at the last and going towards the beginning of the sentence. "Look, Gilray." He held his excitement in. "The first letters – spell them out backwards."

They traced the initials beginning with the *G* of grasp, and then an *R*, followed by *I M O I*. It began the word they sought.

"But unfinished!" Gilray wailed.

278

With swift fingers Nat turned to the title. "Everlasting Reliques," he read under his breath. "That gives us the *R* and the *E*." He was triumphant. "Grimoire!"

Nat raised his head, grinning for Gilray's praise. It did not come. The porkpie hat was bent over the book and Gilray was reading the words whose message they had just deciphered. He repeated them aloud: "Everlasting Reliques. In old magic I retain grasp."

He paused and looked up. "But, Nat," he said, "he's telling us that he holds it still. Even after death he grasps the book."

39

But under heavy loads of trampled clay
Lie bodies of the vampires full of blood;
Their shrouds are bloody and their lips are wet.
— W. B. Yeats, *Oil and Blood*

The headlight beam, as rigid as a boat's bowsprit, angled away from the roadway and nudged into the undergrowth. Nat allowed the car to rock to a halt and switched off. Rain, dripping from the trees, tapped on the roof with uneasy fingers.

"Nat, my friend," Gilray's voice was muffled by the collar of his raglan, "I cannot forgive myself. You should not be here." It was because he blamed himself for Pauline. Ever since he had learned from Nat of what they had done he had spoken of little else, and even now, at the edge of the forest, he wanted to go on alone.

"You are not to blame," said Nat. "I was the one who brought her here."

"But if only I had known!" Anguish choked

Gilray's voice. "If only I had seen!"

"Well, you didn't." Nat was curt; what was done was done and he dared not think of how things might have been otherwise. He got out of the car. There was no breeze, the rain fell in an endless sigh in the roadway and the stars were underseas. He stood still, as if it was necessary to let the cold, wet darkness seep into him, and then suddenly turned to open the car boot. "Who cares!" he said.

Gilray came round the car to stand alongside him. "What if we are mistaken in what we do tonight?" he asked.

"It's no time for doubts," said Nat, but he himself was doubt-ridden. He believed nothing. He had come to the forest in the night only because she had been here. But he saw that the little man was shivering in the cold and the rain and took pity on him. "The grimoire is certain to be where you told me," he said. "He still has the book in his grasp."

Nat lifted a sack from the boot. It was heavy with tools from Gilray's workshop and it clinked as he slung it over his shoulder. Gilray came close to his elbow. "I can go alone," he insisted. "There is no need for you to be there."

Nat shut the lid. There was to be no argument. Gilray was barely strong enough to carry the tools, let alone do what they had planned. But once again the futility of what he was doing rose in him, and only by letting his mind dwell on Pauline was he able to prevent himself turning away. There was no going back. "Don't worry about me," he said.

Their feet sank into the wet carpet of pine needles and they moved silently through the trees until they came to the hidden glade. The pyramid was a dead thing, but a sudden swathe of rain swept across and made it appear to move like the humped shell of a gigantic snail. Loathing gave Nat the courage to step into the open and wade towards it through the knee-high grass.

At the grille in the streaming stonework he found the place where the wire mesh had been torn and he took a crowbar and slashed at it to widen the gap. He stooped again to the sack and lifted out the equipment he needed. The jaws of the bolt cutter were set wide to take the iron bar, but they did not cut, and remained jammed no matter what force he put on the levers.

He stood back, his breath steaming in the cold rain, and watched as Gilray, panting hard, struggled and failed. The little man rested against the wet stone. He was sobbing for breath, accusing himself of weakness. "My time runs out," he said, "feebleness possesses me."

Nat paid little attention. He ran his fingers along the metal bar and felt, at the point where it was bedded in the stone, that it was roughened, attacked by rust. He jammed the cutter head into the rotten base and heaved with all his strength. He felt the jaws bite.

The crack as the bar parted echoed for a moment and then died in the wash of the rain. Nat dropped the cutter and then, gaining a purchase with the crowbar, he leant on it until the iron rod was twisted up and to one side.

He helped Gilray to climb through, and stood alone outside. The rain had increased and the trees stooped in a black ring and leant towards him, hissing as they did so. A touch on his shoulder made his heart jolt, but it was Gilray's hand reaching for the sack. He flung it in and scrambled after it between the flaking bars with fingertips of rain clawing at his back.

"Hell!" he said, and the tomb took his voice and played with it. Against the gloom of the bars he could see that Gilray was still crouching, and then he heard the clatter of iron on the stone floor.

"We have need of this." Gilray straightened and handed him the crowbar. It was clammy from the rain, but the tomb was colder. Nat felt Gilray shiver. "My dear young friend," he whispered, "I fear we have been detected."

Nat twisted once more to the grating, but Gilray said, "Not there." A pencil of light sprang from the torch in his hand and made a circle on the floor. "There," said Gilray. "Can you hear?"

Nat listened. Not an insect scraping with claw or wing case against the stone could have escaped him. But the silence all around them was undisturbed. "There's nothing," he said.

Gilray put a hand on Nat's arm and tried to turn him towards the opening in the bars. "Go."

Nat did not budge. "You need me," he said.

"Quick then!" It was a bark, and Gilray's torch

stabbed into the darkness. It touched the inscribed slab of the burial chamber.

"No," said Gilray. "He attempts to lead us astray with a false tomb. He lies elsewhere."

The light slid across the floor, pausing as Gilray listened, until it reached the third paving stone. "There," Gilray ordered, "and be speedy!"

Nat put the chisel edge of the crowbar to the crack but the stones were too close-set to admit it. He chipped at it gently, fearful of the noise.

"Smash it!"

He lifted the crowbar high and brought it down with all his force. A chip of stone flew.

"Again!"

This time the crack widened and he thrust down into it and heaved back. The stone lunged up and he swung the bar to one side until the base of the stone grated on the floor. He moved the bar and hauled again. The paving stone slid with its own momentum, and the torch beam pierced the blackness beneath. But the space was shallow. No iron rungs led down into a vault. They were in the wrong place.

"Where?" Nat shouted in the broken silence. "Where now?"

Gilray wrenched the crowbar from Nat's grip and at the same time thrust the torch for him to hold. "Stand back, if you please."

The superfluous politeness hung for a moment in the air as they stood, looking down. In the gap where the stone had lain there appeared to be another floor. It was no more than a hand span below, and was grey and level. The torch beam explored and showed there was very little dust but then, sickeningly, Nat recognized what he was looking at. It was a leaden coffin lid that had lain, hugging its corpse in the darkness, down all its secret and festering years.

No one had touched it or was meant to touch. The lead was jealous and clung to its own. A silent coffin, motionless, but Nat, his panic rising, heard a snarl in the hollow of the tomb and jerked back. It was Gilray. He stood like a wild spearman with the crowbar above his head and with a shriek he hurled it down. It pierced the lid.

Nat saw it enter, and saw Gilray withdraw it and stab again. His coat swirling around him, he attacked the lid with a savagery that at first repelled Nat, then drew him closer as Gilray ripped open a jagged hole.

Only the fury that they shared held Nat at the little man's side as from the coffin a reek came forth that put its arms around their shoulders, stroked their necks and stuffed its charnel loathsomeness into their nostrils.

"The torch!"

Nat, gasping so as not to vomit, brought it to bear. He saw Gilray reach forward. He saw his hand vanish through the torn lead. He watched as he scrabbled around in the mess that lay there. And at last he saw Gilray pull back with some dark thing clutched in his fingers.

40

THE UNDERLEAFS

"Underleaf, my darling," said Rosa in bed, "feel my skin." He did so. "Ah, that is divine."

"You are silken, my precious one."

"And my poor fingers have become so smooth."

"As plump," he said, kissing them, "and as delicate as maggots."

"Fie on you!" she cried, laughing. "I wish for a prettier compliment now that I am remade. Something girlish would please me, and then," she whispered in his ear, "I shall tell you something to make you wild with jealousy."

"What would that be?"

"Ah-ah," she chided, "I can tell by your breathing that you are already excited. But first, my pet, you must tell me I am sixteen."

"It is a scandal," said Robin Underleaf, "that I, an evil old man..."

"Very, very evil," she breathed, caressing him,

"and very, very ugly."

"…scandalous that such a vile wretch as I am should take a schoolgirl to bed."

"Ah!" she breathed, "you are stronger than you were, capable of greater wickedness. Kiss this child."

Robin bent to her and did so. "You are young and tender and I shall harm you," he said.

"Divine monster!"

Rustles and sighs in the bedroom caused Robin to become suddenly still. He raised his head. "I hear something," he said.

"Your shoulders are furred like a baboon." She clung to him. "You have a snout and teeth."

His nostrils were turned towards the window. "There is something outside."

"A rat, an owl and an itty-bitty mole. Come to me." He moved as if to free himself from her, but she clutched and held him tighter. "Come down to me," she said, "and let me whisper something that will make you jealous." He paused, and she said, gloating, "I know you and your little ways, my wicked pet. You want to be jealous of little me, so you can hate, hate, hate."

He relaxed and slid down so that his chin was on her bare shoulder.

"I am sweet sixteen," she lisped, "but you are not the first. I met a boy today, and he was lovely."

He attempted to jerk his head away, but she held him. "Don't grind your teeth like that. You frighten me. I'm only a girl."

"Tell me who he was!"

"Ah! You're hurting me!"

"Who was he!"

"Ah! Ah! The pain is killing me!"

"Who!" he snarled.

Rosa was grunting now, her head bent forward so that her chin rested on her chest. "The boy in the shop. He came to see me. He can't keep away."

His words jerked forth, each on a spasm of savagery. "What ... did ... he ... do!"

Deliberately she pressed her soft cheek into the bristles of his face and rubbed against him. "He gave me a gift. A teeny-weeny token of his love."

"What!" The bedside lamp was dim, a softly shaded pink, but it was reduced to a sharp point in the liquid of his eye. "Give!"

She slid her hand from his rough shoulder and reached beneath the pillow. "This," she said, "only this." Rosa's eyes swam in an ecstasy of pleasure as she gave him what he most wanted in all the world.

Half raising himself above her he took the small, but thick, black book.

"It's yours, my love," she murmured.

Resting on his elbows above her he riffled through the leaves, sniffing it. Then he grunted, puzzled.

"Hand written," she said. Her eyes were eager, waiting for the moment when her husband should understand. "The boy broke into the tomb to get it for me. All the magic – all of it, just for me." She

288

caressed herself, goading him. "He lusts for me."

Robin Underleaf arched himself above his wife. In the rosy glow she saw his face. His jaws appeared to have narrowed. His eyes were shaded as if he looked out from fur.

"Darling," she said coyly, "what large teeth you have."

His grunt was composed of slavering hate. She yelped with joyful fear and they lunged at each other, sending the book fluttering out of the bed and across the room like a huge moth. And like a moth it did not escape from the light. They saw from the corners of their eyes that a hand reached out and took it.

Robin and Rosa, joined as they were, moved as one to thrust away from what was watching from the bedside. They moved too violently. Their sheet wrapped their limbs and bound them closer. Their limbs thrashed as if they were lovers in the last throes but their eyes stared not at each other, but at what was gazing down at them.

Long years in the grave had relaxed the muscles of the figure's lips so that they hung open to show the inner flesh and gave him a slack, lascivious grin as he plucked at the sheet and crept in to huddle alongside them.

41

NAT

The Underleafs were not found for a month. On the morning that he heard about it, Nat walked into the alleyway beside the Messenger office. It was December, and old dirty snow silted up the foot of the door of the Shackle Cycle Company. There was no sign that anyone had passed through. He had not seen Gilray since the day the little man had got him to deliver the book to Rosa Underleaf, and the workshop door had always been locked. He pushed at it as he always did, and once again it did not budge. He tried again, but it was solid.

The newspaper had hinted that the Underleafs had lain together so long that there had been difficulty separating them. Until he read of their death Nat had never thought harm may also have come to Gilray. The morning after they had robbed the tomb, the little man had said he was leaving for a while and had solemnly said goodbye before he had handed the book to Nat and given him his last task. In the numb days that followed, Nat had never thought that Gilray might still be in the workshop, and never until this moment that he could be lying there dead.

Nat rammed the door with his shoulder. It threw him back. He lifted his foot and kicked at the lock. Something inside broke, and he lost his balance and staggered inside.

The gloom of December had penetrated deep into the building, and the smell of whitewash was subdued by the coldness of the air. It was as dank and lonely as the tomb in the forest, and certainty grew in Nat's mind at what he would find. Nevertheless, he pushed the door closed behind him. If this was to be the end he wanted to be alone.

He called out Gilray's name as he went forward, but his voice was deadened by the passageway and did not expand until he stepped out into the white space under the glass roof.

"Gilray!" The last syllable went hunting into every corner as it repeated itself, but found nothing.

The bench was there. Nat went close and picked up a spanner. It was like ice. "You were a wizard with these," he said. His cycle was only just beginning to deteriorate from the bright state that Gilray had brought about.

There was a piece of work still in the vice. It was a bar from a cycle frame. Nat loosened the jaws and took it out. Not an iron bar. Black wood. Gilray's walking-stick, but without its silver top or ferrule, and it had been damaged in the middle. An attempt had been made to join it with black tape, but this had not worked well and the stick was too weak to be of use. But Gilray had once made it appear to walk of its own accord, and Nat looked at it more closely. There were two tiny black studs that had probably held the silver top in place, and there were two small holes that could have taken rivets; nothing else.

"I'll take it with me," he said aloud, as if Gilray was there to hear. "It'll only be pinched if I don't." He would keep it until he saw Gilray again.

"If I ever do," he said to the empty space.

He looked into every room of the corridor and they were empty, and he made an attempt to wedge the outer door tight as he left.

The alley was deserted, a dreary space pressed between high walls that rose above him like the pages of a half-open book. The alleyway joined the marketplace at one end, and ran towards the river at the other. Nat did not know which way to go. Pauline was dead. Cassandra and Wheatley were somewhere far away. Gilray was gone.

Only the future was left. He walked towards the marketplace, tapping the ground with the broken stick as he went.

THE BURNING BABY
AND OTHER GHOSTS

~~John Gordon~~

The glowing ashes turned again and then, from the centre, there arose a small entity, a little shape of fire. It had a small torso, small limbs, and a head of flame. And it walked.

A teenage girl disappears mysteriously a few days before bonfire night; two youths out skating see something grisly beneath the ice; an elderly spinster feeds her young charge to the eels... Unnatural or violent death are at the heart of these five supernatural tales, in which wronged spirits seek to exact a terrible and terrifying retribution on the living. Vivid as fire, chilling as ice, their stories will haunt you.

"All the stories include hauntingly memorable apparitions... A major collection."
Ramsey Campbell, Necrofile

ORDINARY SEAMAN

John Gordon

Towards the end of the Second World War, the teenage John Gordon served as an Ordinary Seaman on board a minesweeper. He had some harrowing experiences; coming to terms with the peculiar traditions, practices and language of the Navy was a trial in itself... This fascinating memoir is his story.

TO TRUST A SOLDIER

Nick Warburton

"The rules of war, Mary. You must promise to keep them or it might be the death of us all."

Sometime in a machine-less future, six soldiers – five volunteers and a professional – are on their way to fight for their country against an invading army when they come across a teenage girl, Mary. She becomes their map, guiding them to the battlefield – or so the men are told by their leader, the flinty, dispassionate Sergeant Talbot, whom they trust as deeply as they distrust Mary. One though, young Hobbes, feels sorry for the girl and a relationship develops between them...

"Warburton has a remarkable gift for realistic writing." *The Times*

WEATHER EYE

Lesley Howarth

Telly Craven is a Weather Eye, part of an international youth club that shares information by computer about climatic conditions around the world. And, as 1999 draws to a close, weird things are happening: floods, earthquakes, force ten gales... It's during such a storm that Telly has a Near Death Experience, leaving her with strange psychic powers. Now she is the Weather Eye with a clear, if daunting purpose...

"A large scale story that works, appropriately, through small details that are often very funny... It is subtle, sophisticated and beautifully written... It must reinforce Lesley Howarth's position as one of the best novelists now writing for young readers." *Gillian Cross, The Times Educational Supplement*

"Outstanding... A degree of suspense and pace that would do credit to Raymond Chandler." *The Independent*

THE PLACE BETWEEN

Hugh Scott

"Don't you know The Place Between? That's what I call it... In the darkness, there is somewhere else that comes between me and this world."

Waking late at night, Stella discovers her friend Daniel at her door, terrified, pleading to be let in. The fearful scratching sounds that follow give credence to his tale of haunted woods and creepy scrabbling twigs. Events quickly become even more sinister and dramatic, until there seems to be only one conclusion: some weird supernatural power is at work. A power that threatens to consume anyone in its path...

"Hugh Scott is a master of the genre."
The Sunday Telegraph

THE HAUNTED SAND

Hugh Scott

"Murder, Frisby! Murder on the beach!"

There's something creepy in the churchyard. There's something deathly down on the sand. Darren feels it, Frisby hears it, George thinks it's a bit of a laugh. But there's nothing funny about murder...

"Intriguing ingredients abound: a haunted church; fearful chases; ghostly weeping; skulls; bronze helmets; gems and the Black Death... Rendellesque subtleties of storyline build to an unforeseen climax."
The Times Educational Supplement

SOMETHING WATCHING

Hugh Scott

Beyond the table, something reared. Two tiny dots of light stared at Alice. The thing had grown. In its blackness she saw faint patterns of paw prints on sand...

Alice first sees the leopard-skin coat when her mother is clearing out the loft, ready for the family's move to an old castle – and it makes her shudder. Attached to the coat is a label insisting that it be burned, but without explanation. It soon becomes obvious, though, that something evil has been unleashed. Something monstrous. Something that means the family harm.

"A chilling tale in true gothic style, building to a spine-chilling climax." *The Times*

WHY WEEPS THE BROGAN?

Hugh Scott

WED. 4 YEARS 81 DAYS FROM HOSTILITIES ...
so reads the date on the clock in central
hall. For Saxon and Gilbert it's just
another day in their ritualized indoor
existence. Saxon bakes, Gilbert brushes,
together they visit the Irradiated Food
Store, guarding against spiders. Among
the dusty display cases, though, a far more
disturbing creature moves. But what is the
Brogan? And why does it weep?

"Deftly evoked, the narrative is cleverly
constructed, and there is no denying the
nightmarish power of the story. There is a
true shock ending." *The Listener*

"A very compelling and very interesting
book." *Jill Paton Walsh,
The Times Educational Supplement*

A Whitbread Novel Award Winner
Shortlisted for the McVitie's Prize

ISAAC CAMPION

Janni Howker

"I was twelve rising thirteen, when our Daniel got killed..."

Even before the tragic death of his older brother, young Isaac Campion has a difficult relationship with his horsedealer father. Now the ill feeling between them deepens as does the bitter feud with rival horsedealer, Clem Lacey. It seems as though Isaac's father wants to master Isaac, the way he masters his horses. But Isaac is a boy with a mind and heart of his own.

Winner of the Somerset Maugham Award

Shortlisted for the Carnegie Medal and the Whitbread Children's Novel Award.

"A writer of considerable power of real passion." *The Times Literary Supplement*

"Tough, vivid, convincing."
The Sunday Telegraph

THE NATURE OF THE BEAST

Janni Howker

THE HAVERSTON BEAST STRIKES AGAIN!

The sheep farmers say there's a killer dog on the loose. The children think it must be a monster. The people of Haverston are too devastated by the loss of their jobs to care. But Bill Coward reckons he's seen the beast and he's determined to track it down...

Winner of the Observer
Teenage Fiction Prize

Winner of the Whitbread
Children's Novel Award

Highly Commended
for the Carnegie Medal

"It's hard to envisage a more gripping narrative." *Chris Powling, Books for Keeps*

"Full of feeling, anger and explosiveness." *The Guardian*